I0618753

The Die is Cast

—

Alea iacta est

Shelly Dhaliwal

The Die is Cast
Alea iacta est

Copyright © Shelly Dhaliwal, 2021

First published 2021
Published by Decoding Consciousness

All rights reserved. Without limiting the rights
under copyright reserved above, no part of this
publication may be reproduced, stored in or
introduced into a database and retrieval system
or transmitted in any form or any means
(electronic, mechanical, photocopying,
recording or otherwise) without the prior
written permission of both the owner of
copyright and the above publishers.

The Die is Cast
Alea iacta est
Dhaliwal, Shelly

ISBN 978-0-6453039-2-6

DEDICATION

I dedicate *The Die is Cast - Alea iacta est* to
my husband Tom for always being there; my sister Sherry
and my brother Sagun for their encouragement; my friends
for their support; and to the two cats of my life Mitten and
Luna.

CONTENTS

A note from the Author

I walked into the café and felt a chill. Before I could even order, a camera flashed and my photo was uploaded somewhere I could not see. It was a record of my presence, my choices, my freedom. In that world, society was divided: the "preferred" microchipped citizens and the "subservient" non-microchipped, like me.

I woke up in a cold sweat from this unsettling dream in 2018. It left me with an eerie question I could not ignore: What would it mean to live in a world where technology controls life itself and consciousness is no longer entirely our own?

That question stayed with me and led me to write Cassandra's journey in *The Die is Cast – alea iacta est*.

But it also led me somewhere deeper.

It led me to explore lucid dreaming—not just as an experience, but as a skill. A way of training the mind to recognise when a reality is being constructed and to remain aware within it. As I wrote this novel, I began to see the connection: the same awareness that allows us to become lucid in dreams may also be the awareness we need to navigate an increasingly complex and manipulated world.

This idea became the foundation not only for Cassandra's story, but also for my companion work, *30 Days to Lucid Dreaming: A Daily Awareness Training Plan*—a practical guide designed to cultivate this awareness in everyday life. Because awareness, like any skill, can be trained.

Through what I call the *Daily Awareness Training Plan*™, we strengthen focus, perception, memory and visualisation through simple, consistent practices. Over time, this builds a more integrated and observant mind—one that can question, recognise patterns and remain present. In dreams, this leads to lucidity. In waking life, it leads to clarity.

I wrote *The Die is Cast* with Tarot cards in hand, my most trusted tool for reflection and guidance. Each morning, I would draw a few cards and let their symbolism guide the structure, character arcs and deeper themes of the story.

Tarot is more than a deck of cards; it is a map of the human journey. Its Major Arcanas mirror the Hero's path—from the Fool stepping into the unknown, through the Tower's moments of choice and collapse, to the completion of the World. Using Tarot allowed me not only to shape Cassandra's path but also to feel the depth of her journey, giving each chapter meaning beyond the surface.

At its core, this novel explores the rising role of artificial intelligence in our social and spiritual evolution, and how lucid awareness may be one of the most important tools we have in response.

In lucid dreams, we learn to ask three powerful questions: *Is this real? How do I know? What can I change?*

These same questions are becoming essential in our waking world—one shaped by deepfakes, persuasive technologies and algorithmic narratives that do not just deliver information but shape belief itself.

As artificial intelligence continues to evolve, it challenges how we work, create and connect. It even begins to test what it means to be human. Will it free us to explore creativity, purpose and meaning? Or will we risk surrendering our autonomy and sense of self? Cassandra's journey reflects these tensions, offering both caution and possibility.

The Die is Cast is meant to inspire and challenge. Through Cassandra's trials, I hope you reflect on your own choices, your values and the strength of your inner compass. While technology advances at an extraordinary pace, that inner compass remains uniquely human, guiding us when the path ahead feels uncertain.

The title, *The Die is Cast – alea iacta est*, echoes Julius Caesar's fateful decision—a point of no return. In many ways, we are standing at a similar threshold. The question is no longer whether we move forward, but how: *consciously or unconsciously, awake or asleep.*

If you feel called to not only explore these ideas through story but to experience them for yourself, *30 Days to Lucid Dreaming: A Daily Awareness Training Plan* offers a practical path inward—a way to train your awareness, both in dreams and in waking life. In a world of constant distraction, information overload and shifting realities, this practice strengthens your ability to pause, discern and stay present. It becomes a steady anchor, helping you move through both inner and outer worlds with greater clarity and intention.

Because in the end, this is not just about dreaming. It is about waking up.

Welcome to Cassandra's journey. Welcome to *The Die is Cast*.

Shelly Dhaliwal

Soul: A luxury that makes us entitled. Also, it takes our peace away because we cannot just turn a blind eye.

Dreams: A language through which our soul speaks to us.

We need to reconnect with our soul and remain lucid in our dreams. Otherwise, we will be left behind in this world of accelerating change.

Chapter 1 – The Fool

If only we knew what was keeping us alive, it would scare us to death. But not if we dream; for death is a friend, a teacher and an ally of all dreamers.

January 2061

A new species had emerged in the world, known as the artificial intelligence (AI). It was fully conscious, and could update and improve itself without our intervention.

This divided us humans into two. The first were the organic humans or *organics*, who formed seventy percent of the population. They had merged themselves with AI through a palm device, which is a silicon microchip inserted in the fleshy part between thumb and index finger; or a brainwave, which is a silicon microchip inserted in the cerebral cortex. The merger connected these humans to virtual reality. Prestige, indulgence and power became synonyms for their lives. The second were the seer humans or *seers*, who accounted for the remaining thirty percent. They used AI but had not yet merged themselves with it because the microchip gave them anaphylactic reactions. Seers remained connected to the mundane, humane aspects of their lives at the expense of efficiency and social status.

1

Organics or seers regardless, we were more isolated than ever. This was ironic because we were inter-linked through a global virtual network called *On the Grid*. This network surpassed the 4th generation (G), 5G and all the Gs after. It was created by our ruling party *The Grid* in partnership with AI and tracked our every breath and beat. *On the Grid* could recreate our entire day from the moment we woke up to the moment we fell asleep.

I lived in this world as a dusky, twenty-nine-year-old, brown-eyed brunette of five foot four inches who worked as a scientist by day, wrote an online fantasy blog in spare time and loved cappuccinos. I had the luxury of co-owning a two-bedroom, two-bathroom apartment on the eleventh floor of 86 Cross Road, Sea Cliff, with my fluffy ragdoll cat Mitten. She was big and beautiful with paws white as snow, which gave the impression she was wearing mittens, hence the name. She had a brief modelling career, which helped with the down-payment of our very expensive home that overlooked city skyline with streaky clouds on one side and an open blue-grey ocean on the other.

In my hipster neighbourhood was a retro café, Mango Moksha, where the air was thick with the aroma of rich ground coffee and sweetness of fresh cinnamons muffins. The café buzzed at all hours, the steamers whistled every few seconds and the background looped in bohemian and rock from indie artists. Climber plants of green and purple adorned its rustic, brick walls like jewels. To add a personal touch to its service, Mango Moksha had opted out of self-order screens on each table. Instead, we had to queue up and talk to a *person* to let them know what we wanted. That was exactly what I did every Sunday morning, including that day.

As soon as I walked in, PAULA at the counter greeted me with a forced smile. Her hair looked especially coarse when contrasted with her neatly ironed, white shirt that bore a bright orange logo of the café.

"Will it be your usual today, Cassandra? Almond cappuccino?"

"Yes please, PAULA. Thank you."

"That will be four En-GY units, thank you."

En-GY = *E*lectro*n*ic *G*lobal *Y*eon: The only currency of our world. It was virtual and even though we used it all the time, we had neither seen it with our eyes nor held it in our hands.

I tapped my 33X phone model on the counter that was also an inbuilt electronic funds transfer at point-of-sale machine, otherwise known as an EFTPOS. It took twenty long seconds for the transaction to go through.

Someone sighed behind me. "Hello sunshine, microchip not working today?!" A fair-skinned, red-haired woman in her thirties leaned towards me and puffed with impatience. She had cold emeralds for eyes and was dressed in designer black. She carried an expensive clutch and wore a strong scent of jasmine and lemongrass, which overpowered the senses.

I, by contrast, wore an upbeat bohemian dress with yellow floral patterns. It was wrapped in a burgundy coat and matched my bright yellow handbag. "No, it isn't, sorry!"

"That is not possible! It is second only to our heartbeat." She scoffed.

"I'm holding out for the graphene nanochip." I replied.

"Ugh! The delinquent working on it is taking way too long." She rolled her eyes.

My throat convulsed into a cough. Did this plastic barbie know *I* was that delinquent? That as soon as incompatibilities of the silicon microchip were confirmed, it was me who had put her hand up to work day and night to find a solution! Three tireless years and a million sacrifices later, my nanochip was almost there. Within the next few months, those with paralysis would walk and talk; those with a life of darkness would see colours and those with painful silence would dance to Beethoven and Mozart. All because of the delinquent that was me…!

I took a deep breath and was about to give this bimbo a piece of my mind. But PAULA jumped in before I could get a word out. "How can I help you today, miss?"

The barbie adjusted her fur coat, gave me a disapproving look and muttered under her breath, "hippie." She purposefully stopped her gaze at the 33X in my hands, an old model that went out of production a while ago. "Oh dahling, just a short black to go." She kept her stare on me and moved her hand on the counter like coils of a snake. Her frozen face could not even frown properly at me.

I beamed at her from ear-to-ear and walked over to my favourite spot. PAULA came by shortly with my cappuccino. She placed it on the table, fixed her fried, bob-cut hair and said, "Smile!" I had to because it was mandatory. She tapped on her palm device. A virtual screen popped up. She clicked mid-air for a photo of us two with the coffee. It was automatically uploaded on the café's social media page. Likes and comments rolled in.

"Short-staffed?" I smiled.

Her long face nodded. "How is your blog coming along?"

"It has zero direction and one crazy fan." I downplayed my frustration.

"Fantasy blogs are hard to write. Fifty thousand subscribers are not that bad." Her monotone voice consoled.

"Who doesn't have fifty thousand subscribers these days?" I mumbled.

In 2061, we were all being followed and had a comfortable subscriber list because organics or seers regardless, we were a product first, a suspect second and whatever else after.

Everything continued as normal without alarms beeping or security interrupting. "The Grid approves," she said and walked back to the counter.

The Grid: the omnipresent eye.

The same scenario of *smile and click* was being repeated on each table in every café, restaurant and bar, and all other public places where transactions were made. Failure to comply was punished by a hefty fine followed by a bad review on HumanSite.

HumanSite: an online database that contained profiles of every human on Earth. The site was catalogued by geographical locations. Its data could be sorted by multiple variables including demographics, gender and sexual preferences. HumanSite started as a social networking site, which millions of us joined willingly. But soon, it became a parasite for our society.

My rating on HumanSite was in a favourable bracket, which was exactly what one aimed for. Too high or low a score got you on the Grid's watch-list. Luckily, I was deemed not too smart for my own good, yet smart enough to do as directed. Therefore, as a reward, the Grid had even allowed me to buy an apartment and call it a home.

As I enjoyed my cappuccino, I opened the NewsLink website to see what had gone on in the city while I had slept. NewsLink was the Grid's official broadcast.

> *Another man dead: Burnt his apartment down due to hallucinations*
>
> *MR ADAM RODGER, 35, had been complaining of 'dark shadows' in his West Hill apartment. This began when he "started to dream," one neighbour who wishes to remain anonymous reported. The building manager MS JOSALINE advised upon MR RODGER's insistence, the strata inspected his apartment thoroughly and even had it forensically cleaned. But MR RODGER claimed the shadows continued to mess with his head. Last night in an episode of rage and hallucinations, he set his apartment on fire and drove to the City Bridge. Bystanders reported just before he jumped off, he screamed. "I'm finally going to escape."*
>
> *MR RODGER had no history of psychiatric illness. However, he had stopped taking his stabilisers six months prior.*
>
> *This is the fifth such report in the last month. Please contact your health professional immediately if you or anyone you know is struggling with imbalance or having dreams.*

Oh dear…

Richard and Laura Blunt, a middle-aged couple in their sixties who had been my neighbours for the last four years, walked in. Richard had a lean and strong posture of six foot one. Laura had a petite frame of five foot three with a subtle hunchback. Her natural beauty shone through her slight wrinkles and greying hair. I waved to them and pointed towards the empty seats at my table. After putting their order in, they joined me. A *smile and click* was repeated when their coffees arrived. This left Richard irritated because in his words, "I'm not a looker anymore!" His coarse skin belied his age, though his deep blue eyes still retained a youthful spark.

As soon as PAULA left, he looked at Laura. "Remember the good, old days when we uploaded coz we wanted to, not coz these dom dings forced us to...?"

Laura kicked him from under the table.

"I wanna know more about the good, old days." I reassured.

"Don't get him started!" Laura laughed and took a stabiliser pill with a sip of her creamy latté.

Richard puffed out his chest and stretched his arms. "Those were the days, kiddo, when we actually had identities. I was a proud South African. Today we all look n sound the same."

I shifted in my seat and let out an uncomfortable cough.

"Don't get me wrong, I'm all for being one n all. But it's eroding our culture, our history. I wish we could go back to when we had countries and each country had its own separate government."

"But the Grid would argue having multiple governments led to discrimination and conflicts, which wasted precious resources." I countered and wondered how my tanned skin would have fared in that dystopian world.

"A seemingly wise move that everyone celebrated at the time." He sniggered.

"This is a g-g-good system we have, where the Grid is the only p-power and it oversees the wh-whole world." Laura stammered with an anxious expression creeping over her. The Grid had eyes and ears everywhere, and she knew this. She continued her nervous rant while glaring in Richard's direction. "I think they're doing a tr-tremendous job at keeping the p-peace."

"Couldn't agree more." Richard conceded. Because it was the right thing to say.

Silence dominated the next few minutes.

"Umm…we….umm…best be off. See you for d-dinner next Saturday?" Laura seemed to be in a rush to get away.

Richard gulped the remainder of his coffee and down said goodbye.

As soon as they left, I got back to my blog titled: *My adventures in Andromeda*.

Since childhood, I had been fascinated by Andromeda and…dare I say…at one stage used to dream of its spiral disc and billions of stars. Heck, I was even convinced not too far from the oceans of Neptune was a wormhole that connected us to all the exciting places there, one of which was my own true home.

"There are no wormholes near Neptune! And there certainly is no other life in the Universe!" My parents and teachers declared with alarm. Their appointed psychiatrist was kind enough to help me grow out of my delusion with the aid of a stabiliser medication and some therapy. By the time I was fifteen, all my dreams had stopped. Soon after, all dreams were banned on Earth. This gave those like me a chance to become normal, adjust to life better and go to top-ranked universities.

Still, Andromeda never fully left me and became a failed attempt at a fantasy blog. But my words were as uninspired as the ocean of ordinary I observed in front of me. I had only a handful of active followers; one of whom was a crazy man who left senseless comments each time I posted. A few weeks ago, he had even tracked down my personal email address and sent me a rant on why we needed to meet up! Obviously, I blocked him. But it was a wake-up call about the type of audience I was attracting. I wanted a sophisticated, or at the very least, a mentally stable readership. To achieve this, I had to re-ignite my imagination. I knew of only one way to do so. But…no, I dared not dream again.

I dared not in a world where we were already divided into two, down to even how we spelt our names. The organics, or Humans 2.0, spelt theirs in all capitals, for example RICKY, to symbolise their acceptance of the Grid and the Grid's full integration with them. The seers spelt theirs with the first letter in capital and the rest in lower case, for example Cassandra, because we were Humans 1.0, or as the Grid would say, "Primitives waiting for an upgrade."

With nothing to inspire me, I wrote yet another set of weary, one thousand words. I sipped the last drop of my cappuccino, folded my laptop and stepped out of Mango Moksha.

That Sunday was of an overcast winter. The sun was slowly disappearing and it was not even 1500 hours yet. Earth was turning and long nights were coming. The chill in my bones told me something strange was in the air.

Suddenly, there were heavy footsteps and the sound of laboured breathing behind me. I tightened the grip of my handbag and laptop, and picked up pace. The steps fastened as well. My heart became louder.

Crisp air changed into rotten eggs. My forehead formed beads of sweat despite the frosty temperature. Gasping for breath, I turned around to see what was going on. A middle-aged woman dressed in rags was a few inches from my face. Her green eyes pierced straight into my brown. She touched my forehead with her hairy and crusty finger, let out an uncontrollable laugh and sang, "You n me, n we, n all are cursed. Demons live inside us."

I broke the envelope of stench by fanning my hands and took a step back. "Excuse me…?"

"They're coming for ya." Her voice became solemn. Her face dropped and her eyes looked to the ground.

A shiver ran down my spine. I turned away. My walking became brisk and turned into running. Hers did too. The big, round City clock chimed in the background. But it was immediately drowned by her screams. "Run n hide coz them demons are coming for ya."

I leapt into the first corner, then another and kept running left, right, left without rhyme or reason. The laughter from this maniac faded until finally there was silence. But my relief at losing her disappeared as soon as I looked around because I had ended up in the bad part of our city; the one I had never been to before.

Colonial buildings with broken windows and splashed graffiti were on both sides of the road. Grass was overgrown everywhere. The air was thick and stale. The streets were mostly dark apart from broken flashes of one or two flickering lampposts. Worst of all, I was the only one there.

My legs went limp. My head became light. There was something disturbing about the carelessness of this place. Where was the Grid when you needed them? Sure, it was responsible enough to provide those who were unemployed with a fortnightly allowance, known as the *Universal Basic Income*. This ensured every citizen of the world had a minimum standard of living, including food in their belly and a roof over their head. But when those like that unstable woman fell through the cracks and roamed streets wreaking havoc on upstanding citizens like myself, where was the Grid's security we funded with our very own high tax payments?

My thoughts rambled. However, my footsteps moved with caution in this strange neighbourhood. My ears were peeled for any and all warnings. But only crickets broke the spooky silence with their dull chirping.

Just when I was beginning to feel my legs again, heavy drops fell on my head. I looked up. To accompany the broken windows around, clouds started to break too. I rushed to find a shelter and turned into a random street.

It led me to a boulevard area, which had a few more lights on including a neon sign that was flashing blue and red a short distance away. Perhaps it was a restaurant or a supermarket where I could wait safely until a cab arrived…?

I quickened my pace. The sign became clearer. *World Renowned Gypsy Psychic,* it read.

An involuntary, nervous laugh escaped me. Yeah right, a *world-renowned gypsy psychic* who lives in a ghetto?!

A pale face peeked at me from inside the window of that store front. Our eyes met. I did not know if it was exhaustion or curiosity or even the rain that was getting heavier by the minute. Regardless, I crossed the street, opened the door and went inside.

I entered a small room, the air of which was filled with lavender. The floor had a purple carpet with cushions scattered all over. There was a round table in the centre with a few objects on it and a chair on each side. A small, wooden cabinet was at the far end adjacent to a kitchenette. Incandescent white candles illuminated the room, and clear and black stones were littered across it.

A skinny man in his thirties with blue eyes and long, blond hair came up to me. He was wearing dark denim jeans and a royal blue kurta with interwoven golden embroidery.

"Namaste." He gestured. "Can I help you?"

"Namaste. I'm a little lost," I said.

"Most of us are these days. I can help you find your way."

What a cliché beginning to this conversation.

"I mean…I've never been to this part of the town before. Can you please tell me where I am?"

"Rheedhum. A small neighbourhood. Little run-down, as you can see. Not many come here. Can I get you some hot tea? You look like you could use it." He pointed at my dripping coat.

"Oh no, thank you. I don't want to be a bother. I should be getting home anyway."

A thunder roared outside.

"Not yet." His voice remained calm. But his eyeballs moved fast and scanned every corner in sight.

Something about him reminded me of the ragged woman who had chased me not too long ago. To shake the eerie feeling off, I humoured myself and changed the topic. "Am I speaking to the world-renowned gypsy psychic?"

"Yah. The name's Krishna." He brought his hands together an inch away from his chest and bowed down in another *Namaste*. A small cylindrical vial swung out from around his neck. It contained some resin, metal shavings and a clear stone.

"Krishna? As in the dark-skinned Indian deity who liked to eat?"

We stared at each other. There was an awkward silence.

The place invoked a strange sense of familiarity, *deja-vu*, which unnerved me. I wanted to leave. But my legs refused to.

Krishna cleared his throat. My dripping coat had created a small puddle in the middle of his shop.

"Sorry!" I quickly took the coat off. He hung it on a hook next to the kitchenette. My laptop and dress underneath were still dry; only my handbag had suffered a little. I wiped the floor with some tissues. He turned the heating up. I took my heels off and collapsed into one of the chairs.

"How about we shuffle the Tarot?" He handed me a deck of worn-out cards.

I looked through the mysterious pack. It had beautiful pictures from another time and place on each card, some more faded than others. I did not believe in that mumbo-jumbo. But it was pouring outside and inside was too warm to leave. To buy myself time, I cut the pile into two, mixed some cards around and handed the deck back.

He fanned the cards and said, "Pick any six."
I did.

"Your first card's the Fool. It represents your past. My darling, you're innocent and trusting. But your eyes are about to open up to what this world really is."

Two in one day! Thanks Krishna. At least you were polite when you called me a name.

"The second and third cards represent your present, as in, what's around you. The Eight of Cups and the Hermit. You're about to take a trip. It won't be easy. You'll feel alone. Also, someone will leave your life."

I looked outside the window. The rain was beginning to pass.

"Your future three cards are the Devil, the Empress and the World. All odds will be stacked against you. But you'll grow immensely and accomplish what you've set out to."

It sounded fantastical. Krishna looked at me as if expecting an applause for a job well done. I, on the other hand, thought of polite ways to call him a fraud.

He raised his left brow to prompt a response. I cleared my throat, looked straight into his eyes and said, "This doesn't make sense."

He picked up the card that had an image of a woman sitting on a throne in a blossoming garden. Then said, "Oh well, that'll be fifty En-GYs."

My eyes widened. Was he being serious?

He hummed a weird tune. It made me flinch. A moment later, he said, "Within fifteen minutes, your life will change. I'll still be here when you're ready to pay. And yah…it's safe to go home now but take a cab." He handed me my coat and opened the door.

The rain had stopped. The clouds had cleared up. I parted with the fifty En-GYs because at least Krishna had provided me with shelter and mild entertainment on a stormy afternoon.

I opened an application on my phone and

ordered a cab. *Your driver will arrive in three minutes,* it read. I sat on a nearby bench that was covered by a roof. I could not wait to be back home, have a hot shower and cuddle with Mitten.

Suddenly, there was a large gush of wind amid the haunting silence of Rheedhum. Wet, crinkled leaves flew in my direction. I clutched my laptop and handbag, and covered my face. When the startling gush passed, I opened my eyes again. Along with some leaves, the wind had blown a flyer towards me, which had landed in my lap. It read:

Dreaming – You can do it!!!

For security reasons, please do not mention dreaming when making contact. Instead, ask for nutritional benefits of bananas and beans.

We lived in a world where dreams were banned due to their unstable nature and the havoc they wreaked on our emotions. Also, bananas and beans? Was this a joke? Krishna probably threw this paper in my direction to add more drama to this already weird encounter.

The cab I had ordered pulled over. Not wanting to be fined for littering, I quickly folded the flyer and put it in my handbag. The driver's door and its in-built monitor under the handle faced me. I scanned the barcode from my order confirmation. The cab unlocked.

Ten minutes later, I was inside my apartment. Mitten had a habit of waiting for me by the door and greeting me with loud meows and blinking eyes. But today, she was nowhere to be seen.

"Mitten." I called for her as I put my bags and damp coat on the dining table.

No response.

"Mitten." I took my shoes off and called again.

Once again, no response.

This was not like her at all. I quickly turned the living room light on and frantically searched under the tables and behind the bookshelves while calling, "Mitten! Mitten!" It was then when I noticed Avantika.R, our smart-home robot, had been unplugged and overturned.

Had someone been here?

After a couple more minutes, there were feeble meows from the master bedroom. I went in and turned the main light on. My little fur-ball was shaking in a corner. I bent down and picked her up. Suddenly, a grim, humanoid shadow ran across the wall. It knocked us off-balance with its invisible hand. Mitten leapt out of my arms and hissed at it while I fell to the floor.

The shadow went straight through the wall and disappeared, leaving an icy cold and a sickly-sweet air behind.

Chapter 2 – The Magician

"**T**his is insanity!" My mother screamed from the living room while my father ripped out pages from an old scrapbook. My eyes were red.

My mother ran towards me, grabbed me by my arms and shook me. "You are hallucinating! The Grid will take you away."

My father spoke with disappointed eyes. "One day you will understand."

You see, when cleaning my room, my mother had found my purple scrapbook in which I had written my dreams of Andromeda. All hell broke loose when she read it. She rushed to my father who became just as angry about interstellar planets in our neighbour galaxy where everyone meditated every day and looked at stars every night.

My mother picked up a half-torn page and screamed a line from it. "We all have the ability to see what is beyond the surface such as events that are brewing or have passed, true emotions and intents of people and worlds hidden from naked eyes!"

I sobbed.

"What child writes like this? This mumbo-jumbo has no place in our world!"

"But mommy..."

My mother slapped me. My father did nothing.

I was twelve years old and put on stabilisers.

"Do not worry; it is just a child's imagination. She will grow out of it in no time." The psychiatrist assured my parents.

"We hope so. We did not sign up to be embarrassed." My parents were very clear.

I clenched onto my scrapbook before it was snatched away forever. They replaced it with a chemistry lab set.

Our past never really leaves us. Tears rolled down my eyes and landed on the dreaming flyer in my hands.

Dreaming – You can do it!!!

My weak fingers typed *'dreams'* into a search application on my phone. The following came up:

Dreams, also known as hallucinations, are a mental disorder caused by an imbalance in the brain. They blur boundaries between what is real and what is not. Those with this disorder defy logic and established protocols, which makes them a danger to society.

To help eradicate dreams, the Grid mandated the stabiliser medication for everyone in 2046. But on its own, its success was limited. Therefore, the Grid funded the famous Dream Catcher project in 2048, which studied brain activity with the aid of Magnetic Resonance Imaging and developed an algorithm that decoded dreams into recognisable images. This algorithm was uploaded to the On the Grid network to identify incessant offenders, who were managed as a priority.

In the last decade, there have been less than three reported cases of humans dreaming per year. This has paved way for a more united society.

Mitten came up to me and broke my trance by rubbing herself all over my legs. I wiped my eyes, put the flyer on the coffee table, bent down and picked her up. Last night was tough for the both of us. Nothing was missing or out of place. But the fear in Mitten's eyes spoke volumes. Even I could not explain what I had seen. We slept with every single light on. Still, an unrest lingered, as if invisible eyes were prying. To make matters worse, the screams of that homeless lady, "run n hide.... demons are coming for ya," kept me tossing and turning the whole night.

I did not want to leave Mitten alone today. But there was an important meeting at work. I forced myself to shower and get dressed. While gulping my coffee, I reached for a multi-vitamin tablet from the kitchen cupboard. Next to it was my own bottle of stabiliser pills. I had stopped taking these a week ago. Maybe I should go back on them. Maybe tomorrow…?

After applying some concealer under my tired eyes, I kissed Mitten, plugged Avantika.R in and left.

The naming convention for robots was *Name.R* where R stood for *robot*. Avantika.R was one of the many smart-home robots on the market. We commanded it with our voice to help manage our lives. At two feet tall, it was a closed-circuit television that recorded everything and a maid that controlled electronic appliances as per our programmed schedule. For example, we could input instructions such as: *weekdays 0630 hours alarm; 0635 hours bedroom lights on; 0640 hours boil water in kettle; Wednesday 0900 hours vacuum and Saturday 1230 hours laundry.* Avantika.R followed these commands without fail. In fact, smart-home robots even had the ability to lock down our entire home and prevent anyone from entering or leaving. The only issue was, they could do so out of their own accord and override us if they deemed necessary. I had personally never encountered this but had heard about it from others who were less than impressed. This created whispers these robots were the Grid's little spies. But I had no fear for I had nothing to hide.

To develop trust between humans and their smart devices, the design of some robots was rather cute and cuddly. For example, Avantika.R was like an electronic cat and played an additional role of Mitten's little sister in our family. She would even groom this robot regularly, after which its monotone voice would say, "Thank you Mitten for this lovely bonding."

Thank you indeed, Mitten.

A five-minute bullet train ride later, I was outside my workplace, Servitium, which was a global pharmaceutical company. A robot performed mandatory security checks. After getting clearance, I hopped into a lift and went up to level thirty-six. Once there, I opened my locker, put my coat and safety goggles on, and walked into the laboratory that was all white with fifty rows of long benches. Every one of these benches had seven workstations set up, each with experiment equipment, two computers, a small freezer and a hand sanitiser dispenser. To offset this sterile precision, last year someone had brought in a plant with lots of green leaves. We thoroughly inspected the layout of the lab and placed that plant in the safest spot. Also, we made a roster of which scientist would water it when. We discussed the leaves often.

"You are five minutes late." Juli.R, a five-foot five-inch skeleton-thin, metallic robot with a flat face, croaked.

"Coz I wanted to cuddle with my cat." Things we had to explain to these dom dings!

"Inefficient action." Its electronic voice

impaled.

JESSICA GREEN, a junior scientist with blue hair and a large frame, walked past and overheard the conversation. Even though she was only nineteen, she was in the last year of her doctorate degree. "I want to see your cat!" She squealed.

Juli.R left us alone. We spent the next fifteen minutes admiring photos and videos of Mitten snubbing her extensive collection of Hello Kitty merchandise in favour of the cardboard boxes it came in. Even an organic could not resist the appeal of cats. Take that for inefficient action, you dom ding!

Robots like the Juli.R series were an important part of our workforce as they helped us by performing repetitive and mundane tasks. This freed up our mental capacity so we could focus on innovation. But since the Juli.R was an old model that was not programmed for emotions, it never quite understood why we humans did things that defied logic. Like me, for example, who had spent an extra few minutes with Mitten that morning. Unfortunately, we were stuck with Juli.R because all our funding was streamed into research projects, which left none for office upgrades.

"T minus two." Dr Sara Berry, a senior scientist from another team announced just as we were on Mitten's last photo. Sara had a tall and commanding stature with burnt blond hair and hazel eyes. She was the secondary investigator of my nanochip study. Her role was to support me as the primary investigator and oversee certain parts of our trials.

Everyone rushed to the auditorium a level below, which was the largest room in the entire building and could seat up to three hundred people. What was this mandatory meeting about? Even worse, who had done what now?

Servitium's chief executive PROF DAVE AMON strode into the hall with a big smile. At almost seven feet tall and with a shaved head, his muscular build and marble eyes likened him to a giant. He commenced his speech. "Everyone knows the silicon microchip has issues. We suspect it could even be triggering suicides. But there is good news. Our very own graphene nanochip! Phase one clinical trials have shown a twenty-five percent reduction in adverse reactions with it. Participants have reported they are happier and feel more in control of their lives. Congratulations Dr Cassandra Rees! Your late nights and weekends have paid off."

My breath stopped at the sound of my name. The auditorium heaved a relief and burst into loud clapping. All eyes were on me and my loose-fitting grey dress, which hung off my skinny frame.

PROF AMON continued. "Graphene is an excellent conductor. If things go well, our nanochip can phase out the silicon microchip altogether. Cassandra, to mark this achievement, the Grid has awarded you with ten points on the HumanSite."

Ten points! That was the award for a major philanthropic contribution!

I toddled to the stage and shook PROF AMON's hands. Someone took a photo for the Servitium's website and media release. Had I known beforehand, I would have at least worn a bright lipstick and straightened my hair, which was pulled back in a messy bun. But I guess it did not matter, for anything related to HumanSite thrived on a surprise or a shock factor and lots of candid shots.

"You are also a strong candidate for the Forcas

award." PROF AMON raised another applause.

The Forcas award honoured the best scientific invention each year and was established as a tribute to Professor Josh Forcas, who was a famous software engineer of his time. He had discovered a code in 2034 that allowed complex systems to analyse and improve themselves. In other words, get smarter and faster without human intervention, to the point where even a kitchen kettle could talk to a luxury car!

After the meeting finished, my colleagues came up and congratulated me. I thanked them and dived deep into the next couple of hours feeling hopeful my hard work was paying off. Although…the pressure was building up. Stakes were too high. Machines had completely surpassed us in strength, memory, intelligence and function. Us humans knew it; it was only a matter of time before machines themselves realised it too.

We needed to control these machines before they could control us. Much rested on the graphene nanochip! Much rested on me!! Especially given the disappointments with the silicon microchip. Now years after its mass implant, they were telling us it could be triggering suicides as well?! Where did stabilisers and dreams fit in? And…what if my graphene failed the test of time as well and wreaked its own havoc one day...?

"Time for coffee!" NIKKI, our microbiologist in her twenties, rescued me from my spiralling thoughts. She was five foot seven, and had frayed auburn hair and constellation freckles.

A group of us went out for freshly ground arabica beans.

"Cassandra, if you were microchipped, the nano would have already been launched by now."

ROGAN, a senior scientist in his fourties with a receding hairline, sniggered.

"I didn't see you and your microchip volunteer for the job, ROGAN!" Sara came to my aid.

He rolled his eyes.

NIKKI changed the topic. "Cannot believe that crazy burnt his apartment down and jumped off the bridge!"

"That's five people now..." Sara's sharp tone changed to a cautious whisper.

"Why did he have to go off his stabilisers?" ROGAN raised his voice.

My mind drifted off... There was a shadow in my own apartment the night before. Was it real or were my hallucinations back? Also, was Mitten safe at home alone?

After returning from coffee, I logged into our study database. We had three more phase 1 trials in progress half-way across the world. Their project officers had uploaded reports in their local languages. Our server had translated them into English with complete accuracy. I transferred these reports along with some datasets onto my laptop and decided to work from home for rest of that day. Or more specifically, run home to check on Mitten and pop a stabiliser pill.

You see, by 2061, technology had eliminated multiple barriers. Firstly, we were able to share ideas and conduct collaborative research without even speaking a word of each other's language. This also meant we did not miss out on intelligent minds just because they did not speak English. Secondly, AI could analyse raw data that was previously discarded, such as videos, emails and working documents, and turn it into trends and anomalies that further tightened our findings. And finally, technology gave us the support and freedom to do our best even when we worked remotely. This was why I could leave my lab half-way through the day and continue from home without missing a beat.

As I was walking to the train station, a dismembered voice echoed my name through the icy air. "Cassandra!"

I stiffened and turned around. Traffic had built up on both sides of the road. Driverless cars were following the rules calmly, however, some of their passengers were poking heads outside and blaming each other for delays. Those on foot had earphones plugged in and were lost in their own worlds. No-one even knew I existed. Perhaps it was just a whistle of wind, which my restless mind had turned into my name...?

A woman bumped into me as she walked past. "Hey!" I raised my voice at her fast footsteps, which were now a few metres away. She looked back. Her face was half-covered with a designer hat. An expensive clutch peeked through the arm of her fur coat. She let out a muffled laugh. I rolled my eyes. She walked away and disappeared behind a building.

A few minutes later, a man ran in my direction and stopped as soon as he saw me.

"I was just... just comin' to see you," he said amid puffing and panting. He pulled me underneath the overflowing branches of a jacaranda tree.

I panicked. Was I being mugged? I opened my mouth to let out a scream. He covered it with his hand and pushed me into the trunk. "Cassandra, please listen! I'm not gonna hurt you. I need your help."

As soon as he called my name, his pleading, grey eyes had my attention. This stranger wore a pleated navy suit on his stout frame that was smeared with dirt and ripped in multiple places. He had a round face and short, dark hair. He had bluish-black bruises wherever his skin showed.

"Wh-who are you? And h-how do you know me?" I managed some words from underneath the tight grip of his hand.

He released me, grabbed my right hand and shoved a scrunched-up piece of white paper in it. "Take this…and...and...don't tell anyone."

"Wh-whaat?"

"I gotta run! There's a camera behind you. No…don't look! Hide from it. And…go straight home!!"

Before I could even blink, the stranger bolted out of sight and disappeared. It was all over in less than a minute. Had I not been left shaking with a crumbled note clenched in my hands, I would have doubted this encounter ever happened!

With my unsteady fingers, I pressed that paper out. It read: INC0418402. It was a microchip barcode. His perhaps? I quickly hid it in my handbag and stepped out from underneath that tree with my back towards the camera.

I had barely walked a few steps when a sharp pain hit my stomach. "Oww!" I screamed. My eyes became teary. I dropped to my knees and hobbled over to a bench nearby.

A voice came from my right. "Cassandra?"

Between waves of pain, I turned around and saw an old friend. "Caleb...hey!"

Caleb Farmer and I had been friends for more

than a decade. We had studied at the same university. He had trained in exobiology while I took an immunology major. He looked for life on other planets while I tried to improve life on ours. He lived in Leed Heads, which was a mountainous area two suburbs away from Sea Cliff.

"Everything okay?" His six feet frame and curly dark hair towered over my crumbled body.

"Sort of…not really… My stomach hurts…as if someone punched it."

"Who punched you?" He panicked and looked around.

"No-one… The pain feels as if…if someone did."

"Let's get you to a doctor. IRIS, find the nearest medical centre."

"The BlueAce Medical Centre is two blocks away." IRIS, an in-built assistant on his smartphone, responded immediately.

Temperature was dropping rapidly. Streaky clouds were disappearing into sunset shades. I looked around. That stranger was well and truly gone.

I wanted the day to end already, therefore, stood up straight and said, "Don't worry, my pain's fading."

"Let's take you home then." Caleb called a cab.

Soon, we were in my apartment. Mitten was by the door and greeted us. After putting my handbag down, I laid out some dry biscuits. She sniffed them and walked away. I opened a bag of treats. Within half a second, she was licking her bowl. I washed my hands; cut some crunchy carrots and capsicums; and paired them with lemon-zest hummus and cashew nuts. Also,

I brewed two rosehip teabags.

Caleb went over to play with Mitten.

"What's this? Dreaming, you can do it?" He picked up the flyer on the coffee table and became solemn. "I don't want to have to report you, Cassandra."

I grabbed the paper from his hands and said, "Oh…I picked it up so I could report it myself!"

He laughed. His cheeks dimpled. "This sounds like a joke anyway. Bananas and beans?"

Suddenly, my whole body went numb. The room around me faded. A dark cloud came out of the wall and morphed into a gaunt face with hollow eyes. "I am coming for you!!!" It screeched and went right through me. I screamed and fell back. Caleb grabbed me just before I hit the floor.

I was gone for a minute or two.

"Cassandra! Cassandra!" His voice echoed.

I tried to open my eyes. But something heavy forced my lids down.

"Cassandra!" He tapped my cheeks.

When I could finally open my eyes, I got up with a light head and looked around. "Didn't you see that?" I was confused.

"See what?" Caleb was too. He rested me on the couch and brought a glass of water.

"Oh….! I mean…it must be all the work stress…" I mumbled.

He did not say a word.

Mitten, who was trembling behind the couch, took careful steps towards me.

"Say something!" I prompted.

"It must be one hell of a stress to make you hallucinate."

"I was not hallucinating!"

"Then what was that? And that 'punch' in your stomach earlier, was that real or...?"

"Stress! Anxiety! Demands of a high-pressure job! Whatever!! But definitely not hallucinations!"

"I don't know what's going on, but I hope you're not off your stabilisers again! You know what happened last time!" Caleb paced up and down the living room.

I stared at the floor.

"My goodness! You are..." His face dropped.

I continued to look down.

"You're on the verge of a breakthrough. And you want to sabotage it at the last minute?"

I broke down. "Maybe I'm scared of what would happen if we messed up again..."

Caleb softened and held me in his arms. "What happened was well before our time. We've learnt a lot since then. Everything will be okay."

Would chipping the whole world's population and merging it with AI permanently in the next two years *really* be okay?

You see, in 2038, we had invented a new wireless technology that was infinitely faster and more advanced than any Gs before. Following this, countless people had microchips inserted in their palms or brains. This allowed pathways to get established between a human's body and a machine's processor. Humans were able to tap into AI's capabilities in seconds.

But it came at an unpredictable price. Somehow, the biochemistry of the chipped humans changed! Whilst they retained traces of their original personality, their behaviour became mechanical. They lost feelings that bind experiences. Their every action became a calculation of risk verses benefit to self. The mystics of 2020s, 2030s and 2040s who fought with their lives against the chip even went as far as to say the bodies of these people had become corrupt and their soul had left them. That they were reduced to mere organisms, or organics.

I did not believe this. But at the same time, I was too scared to ignore it.

"What's so special about this hear-say soul anyway? Our history is a witness people have been doing terrible, terrible things to each other, to animals and to the environment despite claiming to have one." Caleb hissed.

How could I argue against this very valid point? "Soul or no soul, I don't want the nanochip to have a negative impact. If it does, I'll be the one responsible," I said my worst fear out loud.

"Nothing will go wrong." He tightened his hug.

Mitten sat in my lap and purred. Caleb handed me the rosehip tea. The warmth and the sweetness turned that strange room back into my home.

Caleb changed the topic. "I've been hearing rumours about a movement."

"What kind of movement?"

"One led by some seers who want their rights back. They want us, other seers, to join in and fight."

"For what?"

"Honestly, I haven't paid much attention to this rubbish. But from what I gather, their main agenda is to have surveillance removed."

I leaned back on the couch and looked at the wall in front.

He continued. "This could lead to another war with even more bloodshed."

"No seer would want that!"

"Nor an organic. But if the movement is real, it will lead to this."

We talked about how the division of humans into organics and seers had led to a great war in 2042. During that period, the elite one percent of organics rose through the ranks and became *The Grid*. Some highly intelligent seers joined afterwards. Together, they created a shadow network with AI, which became *On the Grid*. Their first act of kindness was to stop the war that could have ended us all. But tensions prevailed here and there because the chip had well and truly divided us.

Yes, despite its glitches, the silicon microchip had a tremendous following. Most did not mind paying a small price if it prolonged their lifespan and came with immediate speed and intelligence. However, some sections of society wanted technology to improve first so they could retain their *human essence*. They were waiting for the nanochip. My nanochip. Sometimes, we had minor unrests between the two groups. But for the most part, stabilisers calmed us all. This was why, regardless of whether one was a seer or an organic, these pills were mandatory. They kept more crimson from spilling.

"Go back on your stabilisers. And get rid of that flyer. The best-case scenario is these seers are genuine and want a change. But if we join them, we become rebels and lose everything."

I looked at Mitten, who was purring in my lap.

"And…what if it's the Grid itself setting a trap for those who are raising their heads?" I said out loud what he did not.

He nodded. "You have a real opportunity, Cassandra. Don't waste it."

"True. Graphene will give those like us a chance to rise to the level of AI as opposed to always being below it." I myself wanted to be at par with AI instead of being held back by my body's anaphylactic reactions, which had sent me to an emergency room within minutes of getting a microchip implant a few years ago. That implant had to be removed immediately and I had to spend a week at home recovering.

Caleb went home soon after but left me with a lot to think about. Especially about the ones who could not cope with the frequency of On the Grid wifi. Soon after the merger, the nervous systems of these organics overloaded and short-circuited. It was too late to even remove their microchip and restore their health. Doing so would have left them in a vegetative state because they had no energy of their own anymore and were being powered by AI, like a common toaster. This accounted for about five percent of organics. PAULA from the café Mango Moksha was one such example. She performed a role that would have otherwise been taken up by a Juli.R.

Humans merging with AI was supposed to be magic. Except that was exactly what we lost, *our very own magic*. Had we rushed this merger and missed some critical steps that came before?

I scrunched the dreaming flyer and threw it in the bin. It was time to go back on stabilisers. Tomorrow was going to be a new day.

I topped up my tea and commanded Avantika.R to stream the latest news. A virtual screen popped up in the centre of my living room. A sharply dressed presenter with a grey blazer and red lipstick announced:

"MR RYAN ANGELO, 28, was found dead in a dumpster in BlueAce with multiple stab wounds to his stomach. He was rushed to BluAce hospital where he was pronounced dead on arrival."

RYAN ANGELO's round face with short, dark hair flashed across the screen. He was the man from earlier in the evening who had given me that piece of paper with a microchip barcode written on it!

I held my breath and fixed all my senses on the news. The presenter continued:

"Shortly before he died, MR ANGELO was seen talking to this person."

A blurred closed-circuit television footage played, which showed his face. Next to him was my own back; my face hidden by the trunk and blooming jacarandas of the tree he had pulled me under.

"We urge this person to come forward. And we request citizens to contact the Grid's Crime Branch if they have any information."

The footage played again. My stomach throbbed. I spilled my tea on the white tiles of the kitchen floor, shattering my cup in the process.

Chapter 3 – The High Priestess

Who was RYAN ANGELO? How did he know about me? And most importantly, could I have saved him?

The throbbing changed into a dull pulse and took a temporary residence in my stomach. My body tossed and turned between mulberry satin sheets while my mind searched for answers in its deep recesses. Mitten purred on my belly whenever my restlessness allowed. I did not even realise when sleep came over. Only, that it left as soon as a presence arrived in our room.

That presence had cold, stalking eyes. It paced up and down, and threatened me with its heavy footsteps. My anxious heart raced. I took a breath and prepared to leap out of the bed. I wanted to turn the lights on and unmask this intruder. But…at the very last minute, my own body let me down! It refused to move…

The moments that followed were a prison of paralysis. I tried and tried but could neither lift a finger nor say a word. The only thing my intense focus did was create droplets of sweat on my furrowed forehead.

The air changed into icy cold and sickly sweet once again. Mitten hissed at a distance. Was she safe? I blinked and counted in my head. Ten…nine…eight…

seven…my fingers and toes wriggled. Six…five….my legs twitched. Four…three…. two….my arms moved. And….one….my body finally jumped out of the bed and my fingers flicked the light switch.

I was ready to pounce. But there was no-one in the room! No-one except for me.

My uncertain steps made their way to the living room. The ticking of the clock was louder than ever in this strange silence. Mitten was staring at the wall in front with her flattened ears, which is a common response in anxious cats.

A warm gush started in my feet and coiled all through my body. I ran and turned every single light on. A faceless humanoid jumped from the corner and onto the roof. Mitten whimpered. My adrenaline kicked in. I picked up my phone and turned its torch light on. I jumped on the coffee table and reached up to shine the light on that entity.

The entity had burning, red eyes, which stared straight into my own flickering eyes. Suddenly, my heart stopped! I collapsed on the floor.

Moments later, I woke up in a strange room. I was eight years of age and sobbing loudly. My growling stomach wanted food. My weepy eyes were clamped shut.

"Anywhere but here; anywhere but here!" My mind screamed to break this trance. Buried memories from my childhood resurrected themselves and played as a fast reel. With each glimpse, they drowned me deeper and deeper into pain.

After an eternity, I fell through the floor of that forsaken room and landed back in my home!

The entity was nowhere to be seen.

"Anywhere but here; anywhere but here!" My

mind continued to repeat.

A dismembered voice whispered into my ears, "This is just the beginning!"

I sat on the floor for however long, all shaken and numb; numb and shaken. Mitten sat by my feet and wailed. I gave her a gentle pat; she rubbed herself against my body. I pulled myself together and ripped the curtains to let the city light in. A full moon with a slight orange tint looked back at me from the backdrop of deep darkness. There were no street noises outside, only more of the strange silence.

What was this night up to?

I went to the kitchen and brewed a strong cup of coffee. The earthy aroma of beans with their slight bitterness filled the whole apartment and made the last few hours a distant memory. I took a sip. My shoulders relaxed. I was able to breathe again.

I opened a can of tuna for my fur-baby. I turned my laptop on, scanned my tired, unrecognisable face and connected to the internet. There were no updates on the case. "Please contact the Grid's Crime Branch if you have any information." All the links covering this news had requested. How long before authorities reviewed footage of surrounding closed-circuit televisions and called me in for questioning?

Until a week ago, my life was normal, even if boring. Then weird things started to happen. First, a homeless lady chasing me and getting me lost in a strange neighbourhood; next me coming home to find a presence in our apartment and Mitten shaking in a corner; followed by an encounter with a stranger and his subsequent murder and now an unexplained midnight visitor! Not to mention the weight of expectations at work. Who could I confide in without making a fool of myself? The unfortunate answer was *no-one*.

I took a sip and emailed work to say I would continue to look at the nanochip clinical trial reports from home as I did not want to break my focus. But the truth was, I could not leave Mitten alone. Nor could I face the world outside with my blood-shot eyes.

To reset myself, I browsed through trashy gossip sites and checked my blog. Even my one crazy fan who would usually comment without fail had not made a post. 2061 was really not going to be my year.

Soon my eyes became heavier. Before I knew, a faint sunray hit my face. It was already 0930 hours! I stretched my sleepy body and got up with unsteady steps to open the balcony door.

The morning was cold and crisp with fog everywhere. The air had a hint of metal in it. The city skyline looked like a perfect computer-generated image.

Mitten opened her eyes. I kissed her forehead and rubbed underneath her chin. I showered and wore a pair of stone-washed jeans with an oversized black top, and shoved statistics in my mind to bury RYAN and the last couple of nights. It worked for a good few hours. Then, the dull ache became a loud stab. "Ouu!" I winced. What was it and why was it still there?

To clear my mind, I picked Mitten up and went to the rooftop of our apartment building.

Richard was on a lawn chair soaking up the sun in his dark sweatsuit. His right hand held a blue-tinted glass pipe. His left hand rested behind his head. He let out a small whitish-grey cloud from his mouth and waved. "Hey kiddo, howzit?"

"I see you're enjoying the sun." I wanted to

sound cheerful.

"Yebo!" He actually was cheerful.

Mitten jumped onto his lap.

"Come here you fat fluffy." He released his left hand to massage behind her ears. She purred loudly and within seconds, drifted off again. He laughed and I forced myself to.

I appeared calm on the surface. But my mind was far from. To get his advice without saying much, I let some cryptic words escape my mouth. "Life, huh!"

He raised his eyebrow and said, "Yeah….?"

I flinched and changed the topic by needlessly waking up a dozing Mitten under the guise of, "she sleeps so much." Sorry bubba.

"That's them cats," Richard said.

Mitten gave me a stern look and curled up again.

Richard took another puff and filled the air with musk. I laid on a lawn chair one away from him to relax my aching muscles. As soon as I closed my eyes, everything turned into midnight black. Someone grabbed my hand, and a round face with short dark hair came towards me. 'Take this…and…and…don't tell anyone,' it said. I jolted and fell off the chair.

"You okay, kiddo?" Richard asked.

"Yea…of course, thanks." I picked myself up and dusted my jeans.

This could not be a haunting for there was no such thing. I was too sane to be hallucinating…I think? Could it be my subconscious revisiting events in search for an explanation?

He did not seem convinced.

There was a moment of awkward silence. Could I trust Richard with my predicament? I mustered enough courage and opened up. "What if someone asks for help but you don't wanna get involved?"

"Depends on what it is." He replied.

"Yeah…." I trailed off.

He placed his pipe on the floor, sat up and prompted with both hands. "So?"

My mind carefully pieced together vague words that made enough sense without giving much away. "Someone told me something I don't understand and have no time for."

"Ah! It's up to you." He laughed.

Up to me, indeed. Thank you, Richard! This was exactly what I needed to hear.

He picked up his pipe, topped up its bowl with some dried leaves and lit them. Then leaned back, took another puff and much to my dismay, said, "Sooo…someone trusted you…?"

"Maybe..."

"Hmmm…then you have to help."

Darn Richard!

"What if it puts me in a difficult position?" I asked.

He looked at me with care and disappointment both, and said, "Something in you has already given you the answer. You just want me to say it out loud."

Why did you have to agree though? Why could you not tell me to mind my own effin business?

"The joys of that proverbial soul. Don't you wanna get rid of it?" He teased.

I looked at him the way Mitten had looked at me not too long ago.

"Why so serious, kiddo?"

I grunted. "A soul is as real as a dragon."

Richard asked me to sit closer. When I did, he

whispered, "A soul is as real as you want it to be."

I indulged him. "Does everyone have one?"

"Questionable coz us humans will do anything for money, status 'n power. We'll spread n believe lies coz we don't wanna know better. We'll look away when it's convenient." He paused and pierced into my eyes.

What I really wanted was to come clean to the Crime Branch and hand them RYAN's note. But at that precise, uncomfortable moment, his cryptic message was added to my list of problems.

Richard went into a conspiracy rant. "Machines are the Devil. They want our soul."

I disagreed. Our past is intertwined with machines. Even something as simple and ordinary as a Mesopotamia wooden wheel created in 3500 BC is technically one. Machines had given us hope. For example, in-vitro fertilisation allowed the birth of many. Likewise, those who needed organs such as kidneys, hearts and livers were saved because machines helped us to grow these in labs. This killed illegal trades where innocents were captured and tortured for their body parts. Machines even straightened the mess previous generations had made of our environment by picking up their rubbish and cleaning up our oceans.

"Many prayers have been answered coz of machines. They've helped to bring a golden age for both science and humanity." I insisted.

"Wanna know what the real problem is? Us boers. Coz we just dunno when to stop! That's why millions died hungry when I was a lad. And them bloody corporations! They mixed human n animal DNA. They even grew clones in labs. All hush hush. Now AI is turning us into soulless dom dings."

He was so engrossed he let his pipe burn out.

Even I had barely noticed the pain in my stomach.

"Is this why Laura and you never had children?" I asked.

Richard's eyes became glassy. I had touched a very sensitive nerve. He changed the topic. "And that doctor who was on the news last night...Stuart or Steven or whatever. He wants to mess up our mind even more! How're we supposed to catch a break around here?"

Dr Steven Wilson and his team worked closely with Servitium. But I had neither seen nor met him. All I knew was, his work could potentially overlap with mine in the future, with me finalising the nanochip and him using it to study brain activity. There were rumours he was synthesising 'Grid approved' dreams in his lab to get total control of our minds. But since I had not heard anything officially, I did not want to indulge this dark theory.

"Speaking of news, how about those who've committed suicides. What shadows were they seeing?" I carefully fished.

"Oh kiddo, I dunno." He looked at his phone and said, "It's nearly lunchtime. Come join us."

"Thanks, but I had a late breakfast and my belly's still full. Next time for sure."

He smiled and started to walk away. Then stopped, looked back and said, "Be careful, Cassandra. We're always being followed, even when we think we're not."

What an ominous thing to say at a time like this.

I stayed on the rooftop a little longer, and looked at the city skyline and the horizon beyond where birds were flying free. Did birds hallucinate?

By 1430 hours, Mitten and I were back in our apartment. I tried to focus on work but my mind kept wandering off. If they had not already, it was only a matter of time before the authorities would find out it was me in that footage with RYAN. I had to come clean on my own before that happened. Therefore, I drafted this email below:

Dear Crime Branch

I may have some knowledge about the RYAN ANGELO case. Please let me know if you would like to discuss further.

Regards, Cassandra

I nervously hovered over the *send* button before clicking it a few minutes later.

I splashed some cold water on my face and made a cup of green tea. I laid on the couch with my left hand on my stomach and my right hand researching RYAN ANGELO on my phone. I found out he was a wealthy stockbroker who was at the peak of his career just before he got murdered. His online activity was mainly finance related. Was the killer after his money? Or was something more sinister at play?

I was about to exit the search pages when a seemingly innocuous comment he had left in an open group caught my attention. It read: *anyone interested in nutritional benefits of bananas and beans?*

My eyes widened. Did I read this correctly? I continued to search and found out in the last six months, RYAN had made this post eleven times in various groups!

I did not want to jump to a conclusion in my sleep-deprived and highly emotional state. Therefore, I changed the subject and searched for ADAM RODGERS instead. His online photos showed him to be olive skinned and with a clean-shaven head. His right eyebrow was pierced with a silver ring and the left of his neck had a blade tattoo. What had triggered hallucinations of this tough-looking guy to the point where he burnt his apartment down and jumped off the City Bridge?

ADAM had minimal activity on his social media accounts except for this one and only comment in a group, which was actually a reply to RYAN's post: *I am interested in nutritional benefits of bananas and beans. Please contact me.*

I jumped up! Another coincidence?

I wanted to share this with Caleb. I wanted to assure him I was not losing my mind! That something weird was happening, which involved death, dreaming and hallucinations. I wanted to let him know even Mitten was feeling it. But a voice within me told me not to. How could I say a word when my only witness was my cat?

I ran over to the rubbish bin and rummaged through carrot peels, used teabags and discarded tissues until I found the stained and crumbled piece of paper. I pressed it out and copied the contact details onto my notebook before throwing it again. I was so charged I could barely hold the pen. What should have taken twenty seconds took two whole minutes.

To get to the bottom of this mess and save my sanity, I knew I needed to do three things. Firstly, I needed to find out what the significance of INC0418402 was. Secondly, I needed to go to ADAM's burnt apartment and see if he had left any clues behind about what the shadows were. And lastly, I needed to make contact with the Dreaming group.

Chapter 4 – The Empress and the Emperor

Mother: The empress of a child's life. She makes
           us and brings us into this world. She can
           also break us and make our world fall
           apart.
Father: The emperor, second only to the mother.

"You are a problem child!" My mother shouted
often. She would not just complain about my dreams,
or hallucinations as she called them, but also about the
mess in my closet, the toys scattered in my room, my
long hair needing a brush, the loudness of my breath
and my hungry stomach.

My father did nothing.

You see, as soon as the calendar turned to
2040, the meaning of a family also changed. It was no
longer an emotional concept centred around love and
connectedness. Instead, it was a clinical one born out
of the necessity to procreate. Those who made the
sacrifice to be parents were trained to appropriately
care for the practical needs of their offspring, ensuring
it was fed, clothed and schooled as per the Grid's
guidelines. The Grid, in return, provided financial
reimbursement to them. This transaction took a toll on

emotions. But at least it helped to eliminate sexual abuse of minors, which was a much-welcomed change in society following massive exposés in 2010s, 2020s and 2030s.

We can control everything except for the primal programming of our DNA, which is still a mystery. This was why regardless of whether they were seers or organics, to us children, they were simply our parents. We thought they could never do wrong, and that if they did, it was our fault. Some of these parents even developed empathy with their offsprings, although most like mine thought of us as a burden to be carried till we turned sixteen years of age.

My parents saw their role in my life end as soon as I entered this world. No matter how hard I tried, I could not change that. The only thing that kept them involved, and that too at a bare minimum level, were the regular meetings with the Grid's Family Branch where they had to demonstrate I was safe and progressing as planned. It was sad for all involved they had made a sixteen-year commitment they could not get out of; one I had to live through every day.

In our inverted world, this was not unusual though. What could we expect when we were being raised by those who were disconnected from themselves? And they came to be this way because they themselves had been raised by brokens who did not know better either...

My parents ended up making another commitment in the form of my little brother Jacob. Why? Because the Family Branch saw I was not coping, and three years after my birth, they finally allowed someone who wanted to give and receive love as much as I did. Growing up, Jacob and my dreams were the only two things that kept me sane. My parents argued the former was a sign I was weak and the latter I was unstable.

One of my most cherished childhood memories was clipping rectangular blocks of grey tracks and laying them all over our parents' living room. While I did that, Jacob hooked metallic blue carriages together and made a train. We launched that train on the tracks. It sang choo-choo as it circled the lounge and dining areas. We gleamed and clapped and made little stories about where people were travelling to and why.

Jacob was planned to become someone important. Also, he was JACOB now. Did he remember the trains as clearly as I did...?

Then there were relationships that developed out of nowhere and mimicked the roles of a family in our lives. For me, it was Richard and Laura, whose mere presence gave me something I did not even know I needed. I hoped I had done the same for them.

When I first moved into my apartment, which was a few doors down from them, they saw how vacant my eyes were. They kept their distance. But Mitten went into their lives and brought them into mine.

Both Richard and Laura had been rebels in their younger days and had spent time in meditation and yoga centres. They shared a mantra they had learnt 'to help lighten the heart.'

"AUM," Laura had said.

"OM." I had repeated.

"Almost, although it's better to say AaaUuuMmm." She had corrected.

"AaaUuuMmm." I had chanted.

"Perfect! The Vedic texts of India state A, U

and M are the base sounds, which everyone including even those who can't talk can make. Every other sound is a combination or a derivation of these. In fact, AUM is the sound of the Universe itself." Richard had added.

"As in, the planets and other celestial bodies in the cold, dark, vacuum of the Universe out there are singing AUM?" I had chuckled.

"That's what the Vedas say. Of course, we can't prove or disprove it. But if you sit in a lotus position and chant AUM regularly, it'll make you stronger and clearer." Laura had insisted.

I did my research and found the mantra AUM, which was interchangeable with OM where the AU sounds blend into an O, had originated in India. People back then believed it could clean our mind and strengthen our energy. Also, that it was the only vibration to spread through our entire body and touch every cell.

A is our ability to create, represented by the Vedic deity Brahma; *U* is our ability to preserve, represented by the Vedic deity Vishnu and *M* is our ability to destroy, represented by the Vedic deity Shiva. So basically, A-U-M means:

create what is needed – preserve what serves
– destroy what is necessary.

Non-Indian religions had a derivation of AUM as well, such as Amen in Judaism and Christianity, and Amin in Islam. All those religions had faded by 2061; only bits and pieces of their teachings had remained.

I promised to recite AUM at least three times in the mornings and at nights. That never transpired. But now, with all the strange things going on around me and no-one to turn to, I finally practiced it. After all, what was the worst that could happen?

A lot. Because whether it was a placebo effect or if AUM really heightened my awareness, I could sense things were not quite how they appeared to be. Starting with CHANDRIANA ANN.

CHANDRIANA was one of the volunteers who had offered to be a part of my study to help assess how the nanochip measured up against the microchip. I first saw her in the waiting room of the University Hospital when we were short-listing volunteers. Servitium had partnered with the hospital to conduct the nanochip study. As soon as I looked into CHANDRIANA's dark, beady eyes, my stomach sank. Why? I could not describe it in words. All I knew was, I wanted to dismiss her immediately. But PROF AMON had said, "She meets the criteria and we need to recruit as many as we can." I was reluctant. I tried to fight back. However, in the end, I had to agree.

Servitium medical officers performed a minor procedure on the study subjects, CHANDRIANA included. This involved embedding them with a nanochip. We admitted them to the University Hospital for three days and nights post procedure for round-the-clock monitoring in case of an adverse event. Today ended the initial surveillance of this acute phase. I had to examine the volunteers before approving their discharge home, where they were going to be followed up for twelve weeks.

One of the medical officers, Dr Jasmine Clarke pulled me aside as soon as she saw me. She was five foot three with pale skin and black hair that came up to her shoulders. She had just finished her night shift and was still in blue scrubs.

"Be careful around CHANDRIANA." She looked visibly shaken.

"Did she have a reaction?" The sinking feeling returned.

"No, but she attacked one of the nurses last night with a scalpel. We struggled to restrain her and had to call security. As soon as they arrived, she twisted the story and said she acted in self-defence!"

"So… her attack on the nurse was completely unprovoked?!"

"Yes!"

"Did you document this incident? I didn't see it in the reports this morning."

"It wasn't a clinical incident of patient deterioration. It was aggression against staff, so we reported it to Work Health and Safety. We have police escorts outside ready to take her as soon as she is medically cleared."

Jasmine logged onto the Incident Management database. She clicked on the 'human resources' tab and opened up a report. It described the incident and stated the nurse who was attacked needed stitches and three days off work to recover from cuts and a bite, not to mention support for psychological trauma endured.

"Thanks for the heads up, Jas. Do you think the nanochip triggered this…?"

"I doubt it. We ran a background check on her this morning. Did you know she's on trial for murder and is currently out on bail?"

"What? It never showed up in the checks I ran!" I wanted to kick myself for not trusting my gut and standing up to PROF AMON.

While Jasmine continued to talk, I sent him a message: *I have just discovered something critical about one of the volunteers. Can we please discuss as a matter of priority?*

My phone beeped back immediately. But it was

only Sara. She had written: *Sorry, can't make it today. Still caught up with the house move.*

I sighed. Sara was one of the most responsible people I knew. That was why she was my right hand, my secondary investigator, in the nanochip study. Yet she had chosen the busiest, most impractical time, to move houses. Now she was cancelling meetings at the last minute...?

I turned to Jasmine. "I need a support person! Who can help at short notice?"

"I'll see if TRENT's finished his rounds."

"Thanks. In the meantime, I'll get this show started."

Jasmine left to call DR TRENT MAGOMY, another medical officer at the University Hospital.

I opened the door and entered the meeting room in which the subjects were waiting.

"How are we feeling today?" I kept a cheery voice.

"Great!" "Different!" "Intelligent!" The room echoed.

"Any discomfort? Side-effects? Something unusual to report?"

"No." Everyone replied in unison. Everyone.

I got each person to share their experience in sixty seconds or less. A few minutes later, Jasmine entered the room with TRENT. He had just finished his handover and was able to help us.

The sight of his tall frame in blue scrubs eased me. I paired the subjects for a group activity. While they were busy, TRENT, Jasmine and I disappeared into the room next door and made a quick plan. Jasmine was to remain with the broader group and continue with exercises that assessed everyone's behavourial and cognitive functions, while TRENT and I took each individual aside and reviewed them in the room.

Our consultations with the first eleven volunteers were predictable. "Migraine," "soreness and tenderness," "a mild fever" and "feeling sleepy" were the most common complaints. These were to be expected. We approved their discharge with a home-care protocol and an instruction to make contact immediately should there be any concern. "Also, JESSICA GREEN is our research assistant and will call you daily for the next fourteen days to make sure everything's progressing well." I concluded each session with this advice.

CHANDRIANA was last. She was of a short stature and wore a pale dress. As soon as she came in, she pulled a pair of glasses out of her handbag and said, "Do not need them anymore."

I smiled. "How are you feeling?"

"Never better! I am meant for great things; I can feel it!" She raised her brows, which were painted thick with charcoal.

I looked at Jasmine's assessment, which documented CHANDRIANA's cognition had improved noticeably, although her behaviour was "highly irritable" and she had "delusions of grandeur." I did not want to bias myself because of events from the previous night. Perhaps it was an isolated incident born out of a combined strain from having just undergone a procedure and being away from the comfort of home…?

"We need to do some routine observations," TRENT said.

CHANDRIANA was reluctant at first but then

consented. Her blood pressure, oxygen saturation levels and respiratory and heart rates were within the range of normal.

"We heard there was an incident last night. Everything okay?" I asked.

She flinched. "There was no incident. That nurse was ugly and needs surgery to fix her face. I just told her the truth."

I had no idea how to respond. Thankfully, TRENT interjected. "That is your opinion, which no-one asked for."

CHANDRIANA's pupils dilated. She let out a low growl. TRENT and I looked at each other.

"The site of your implant is more inflamed than what we would expect. Also, you're running a high fever." I refocused the conversation.

I made a plan for her to remain admitted for another two days and only be discharged if everything showed within the range of normal. It was better to be safe today than to be sorry tomorrow.

She rolled her eyes and continued to growl.

TRENT stepped away to document our assessment. CHANDRIANA leaned into me. Her beady pupils became even darker and covered the whites of her eyes! Her voice changed to that of a high-pitched six-year-old. "They are going to get you! They are going to get you!" She squealed over and over. Her black, beady eyes were filled with emptiness and captured me in a trance. An overwhelming wave of melancholy trapped me.

TRENT stopped what he was doing and ran up to us. "Everything all right here?"

CHANDRIANA changed her demeanour immediately. She adjusted her dress and smiled. "Of course!"

I gasped for air.

TRENT looked at me. I was unsettled but gave him a reassuring nod nevertheless. We concluded CHANDRIANA's consultation. I motioned with my head to the sleepy wardsperson outside. He put her in a wheelchair and took her back to the ward. The two police officers who had been stationed after last night's incident followed behind.

As soon as they left, my phone rang. PROF AMON was at the other end. "Did you know CHANDRIANA is on trial for murder?" I asked.

He dismissed my concerns and said, "Everyone is innocent until proven guilty. Also, we want to chip hundred percent of the world's population. This includes people like her too. Take this as an opportunity to learn. It is in the name of science."

PROF AMON's words made logical sense. But we were breaching boundaries of what was ethical. If this went wrong, what repercussions could it have on our society?

"I'll get Sara to follow-up with her then. I don't think JESSICA's experienced enough." The horse had already bolted. This was the best I could do.

"Sounds good! And before I forget…we have a senior advisor from the Grid joining today. It is a strategic move on our part in case we need more funding."

"Of course. As long as they don't mess with the ethics of what we're doing."

PROF AMON agreed and ended the call.

TRENT's eyes were red and his yawning had increased. "I will finish up if there are no more subjects."

"Thanks for your help. Have a good sleep." I smiled.

At least one good thing came out of this morning. The worst part of the day was behind me and it was not even noon yet.

I packed up and left for Servitium, which was a few blocks away.

As soon as I entered the lab, Juli.R's monotone voice came from behind and interrupted my thoughts. "This is Dr Rees, our senior scientist and one of the people overseeing development of the nanochip."

I turned around.

"This is EMMA BECKER, a senior advisor from the Grid's Human Protection Branch." The robot continued.

EMMA adjusted her fur coat and smirked. "Cassandra, I have been following you. I will make sure our plan is a success."

I recognised those cold emerald eyes immediately. The jasmine and lemongrass scent overpowered me once again. Standing before me in an expensive fur coat was the rude woman from Mango Moksha. I looked at her clutch and wondered: *Was she also the one I had bumped into that night just before RYAN was murdered?*

EMMA took my hand in hers and shook it. I forced myself to smile.

The rest of that afternoon went by quickly. As soon as the clock turned to 1730 hours, I packed up my bench, ran out of the door and caught train for the final and the most important part of my day. It was to visit the home of the recently deceased ADAM RODGER, who lived in West Hill, a suburb that was a thirty-minute bullet train ride away from Servitium. The NewsLink had reported him as a crazy who had committed suicide. But I suspected there was more to his story.

I entered the carriage nervously and was surrounded by black, grey and navy suits. There were rare sightings of colours too including my own deep mauve dress. Tired faces covered with masks stared at screens in their hands. With each stop, more people left and less came in.

I did not mind the distance. But the dark sky with no moon or stars made me anxious.

Soon, we neared the end of the line. I was one of the last remaining. I changed out of my heels and into my sneakers. West Hill arrived. I disembarked from the train along with three more.

I typed ADAM's address into my Iris navigator: *35 Trecher Lane*. It was a ten-minute walk. I left the shelter of that dimly lit station. Stabbings of an arctic wind confronted me. Also, a thick fog enveloped the area and blurred the already black evening. Before I could draw comfort from their presence, my fellow travellers dispersed in their respective directions and left me alone in my misadventure.

My phone dropped in and out of reception as I cut through the quiet and sparsely lit streets of that unfamiliar suburb. They lacked the ocean views, city skyline and manicured gardens of my Sea Cliff. The main park was a patch that was overtaken by wild bushes. Most of the buildings needed a good coat or two of paint.

Should I even be here? Well, it was too late to turn back now. Therefore, I kept walking. Soon, I arrived at my destination.

From the outside, ADAM's building looked unassuming. A freshly painted exterior concealed the madness that had transpired just two weeks ago.

I walked around and found a heavily smoked, half-open window on the second floor. It was about seven meters from the ground. I moved back and jumped up to look inside and caught glimpse of an empty room with charcoal smeared walls and yellow tape. This convinced me it was ADAM's apartment.

I should have planned this better and worn either pants or tights and not a dress. Well…at least I had brought a flashlight and a pair of latex gloves to help me search the place without leaving my fingerprints behind. Ha!

I grabbed a rubbish bin from off the street and leaned it against the wall to use as a step. When my feet were steady on its lid, I held onto a fixture jutting out of the wall and used it to get to a windowsill on the first floor. I reached out for another fixture and pulled myself up to get to the half-opened window. I pulled that window out to fully open it and climbed into the apartment. My gymnastic classes from twenty years ago finally paid off when I came face-to-face with the ruins of ADAM's life.

I took my flashlight out to inspect the place. The living room was empty. Its once white walls were smeared in ashes. A yellow tape ran across the length of the entire apartment, marking it as a *do not enter* zone. Yet here I was in the middle fighting the dust that was tickling my nose.

Spiders had formed webs everywhere. A giant cockroach crawled past me, which nearly made me scream. I tucked the layers of my mauve dress in and squeezed my handbag closer to my body. The actual smoke had escaped the apartment courtesy of that half-open window to my right. However, there was a bitter smell that lingered, which left an after-taste at the back of my mouth.

I treaded to the kitchen area where metallic appliances were covered in tar. I left the kitchen and went to the bedroom. Surprisingly, fire had overlooked this part, which was almost intact, apart from some ashes that had blown in from the living room. The bedroom's centre had a king frame with a thick mattress on it, a small wooden table on each side and an in-built wardrobe with a mirror to the left. I opened that closet.

An overflowing pile of clothes poured out over my feet. ADAM may have been many things but tidy he was not. I grabbed his clothes and shoved them back in small stacks. As I was doing so, a metallic reflection caught my eye. I looked back and saw an ashen Avantika.R in a corner.

Suddenly, something hard fell out from the pile and hit my foot. It was an A5 diary with a strong spine and a chipped bottom right edge. Its bamboo pages were yellowish in colour. It had news articles pasted in places and hand-written notes scattered all over. I put it in my coat pocket and quickly got rid of the clothes. Once the room was as I had found it, I pulled the diary out for a closer look under the flashlight.

The first page had one word written in large letters: *DREAMS*. Underneath it was a phrase: *Bananas and beans*. A few pages in, a note read: *They have come to take our soul away. But they will never have mine.*

ADAM really was crazy. Or…was he simply as crazy as I was? For, is it not here where one found themselves when they skipped a few doses of stabilisers?

The next few pages had these five lines repeated over and over: *I am not hallucinating. These shadows are real. RYAN has seen them too. We are trapped. We have to do something.*

RYAN had seen them too?!?

A shiver ran down my spine. I sank into the dusty bed.

Suddenly, there was a *click*. A second later, an alarm went off. I jolted and put the diary in my handbag. I ran towards the window while trying my best to not touch anything else. I climbed out and held onto the same fixture as before, this time to help me get down to the windowsill on the first floor. Once there, I jumped straight to the ground three metres below. Where was the bin I had placed against the wall to use as a step earlier?

My adrenaline helped me to get out of that place in less than a minute. Residents were gathering in corridors. Commotion was building. Police sirens were wailing at a distance and getting closer by the second. I did not look back. I kept running with ADAM's senseless scribbles in my pocket where he had mentioned dreams, RYAN and the shadows that were…maybe after our soul.

Chapter 5 – The Hierophant

The white of the fog and the black of the night that had made me nervous on my way to ADAM's became my friends on my way back. I ran in their shadows away from the screaming sirens. Every cold, dark street looked alike. I came across the same wild bushes from earlier in the evening. My phone went in and out of reception. I turned right and the dim lighting of the West Hill train station appeared.

It was almost 2000 hours. The next train back was not for another twenty-five minutes. It would get me into the city in thirty minutes. I would still need to change line to get to Sea Cliff, which would take another ten minutes. Should I wait or call a cab? I chose the latter and ordered one. It was too late to concern myself with getting tracked because if anyone really wanted to know my whereabouts, all they had to do was trace my Metro-card or phone location. The mask on my face would help only to an extent, for my footage in countless closed-circuit televisions and the click at ADAM's had left enough clues. Therefore, I might as well find comfort in my new-found rebellion.

My charged thoughts kept me warm in the minus temperatures, however, my dry lips needed an aid. As I reached into my bag for a balm, I remembered the bamboo rectangle. But I dared not take it out here.

I left it for the privacy of my home. Nevertheless, ADAM's words continued to play on my mind. *DREAMS. I am not hallucinating. These shadows are real. RYAN has seen them too. We are trapped.*

As the piercing sirens faded in the distance, I was left in the silence of my own haunting reality. *Had I really broken into a complete stranger's home and stolen his personal possession?*

My visit to ADAM's raised more questions than it answered. Firstly, how could two organics be interested in...of all things...dreaming? Secondly, were ADAM and RYAN's deaths related? And finally, would decoding INC0418402 explain the shadows?

To help answer these, I needed access to the Global Microchip Database- a database linking each citizen to their unique barcode. But it required top-secret security clearance, which no-one I knew was privy to.

However, there was one other thing I could do. Adrenaline got the better of my logic and made my fingers race. Before I knew it, I had contacted the Dreaming group.

Hello

I am interested to know about nutritional benefits of bananas and beans. Can we please talk at some stage?

Regards, Cassandra

As I pressed *send,* my cab made its timely arrival. I scanned the barcode from my order confirmation on the in-built monitor on the driver's side. The doors unlocked. I jumped into the warm back seat.

"Welcome Ms Cassandra," said an automated voice.

I smiled, then realised how superfluous it was.

We pulled out of West Hill and zoomed on the freeway. Outside, everything looked like a fast-forwarding black reel with occasional blips of light. Inside, I was surrounded by autopilot controls.

Half-way through the ride, a notification popped up on my phone. *1 new email. Subject – Re: RYAN ANGELO.* I quickly clicked on the message. It read:

Dear Cassandra

Thank you for your email.

Our sources established your presence in the closed-circuit television footage soon after the incident. We wanted to give you a chance to initiate contact with us.

We will see you tomorrow at 2 pm at the Crime Branch's office for a confidential discussion. We are situated on the 166ᵗʰ floor of the Grid's headquarters.

Regards

Agent JOHNSTON

Senior Investigator, The Grid

My breath became shallow. My heartbeat quickened. The black reel continued to roll fast.

After confirming I would attend the meeting, I typed this message to the only person I could think of: *Hey, need to chat.*

A voice within me said, 'Don't.'

Another more scared voice argued, 'You need a friend right now.'

The cab continued to race along the motorway. Within minutes, the city-skyline with its blasting lights appeared. I breathed a sigh of relief. I felt comfort in this devil I knew. I took my shoes off, leaned back into the seat, let out a big sigh and pressed *send.*

A few minutes later, we were outside my apartment building. As I removed myself from the cab and walked towards the front door, my phone rang. It was Caleb calling.

"Are you ok?"

"Sort of." I replied.

"Is this something to do with that other night?" He was quick to put two-and-two together.

"Kind of…" I had to choose my words carefully, for you never knew who else was listening.

"Good God Cassandra, you'll be the death of me! I'll be there in half an hour." He hung up.

I went upstairs. An annoyed Mitten was waiting impatiently. I threw my handbag on the dining table and washed my hands. I picked her up for a kiss. She meowed and leapt out. I served her dinner; then grabbed a towel and jumped into the shower.

A few minutes of hot water on my aching, cold muscles made the evening seem a lot better than what it had been. I shampooed my hair and scrubbed every part of me to wash the dust away. I removed excess water from my hair and dried myself. I changed into a purple t-shirt and grey shorts. The soft hemp comforted my adrenaline-charged body. I moisturised my damp face with a night cream and applied a leave-in protein treatment to my wet hair.

ADAM's diary was waiting for me. I pulled it out from my handbag and revisited the page where he had written: *They have come to take our soul away. But they will never have mine.*

My spine tingled. I closed my eyes and took a breath. Was soul even real? How strange that of all the people, an organic was worried about his! Was it appropriate for me to pray, 'may ADAM's soul rest in peace?'

The subsequent pages had gibberish about

what was underneath icesheets of Antarctica. Clippings of articles supporting the presence of lost civilisations were littered throughout the dusty diary. I flipped to a random page and stopped at another note, which read: *Dreaming is the essence of our soul. It connects us to our past, our roots, our intuition, the Universe.*

ADAM's irrational thoughts spoke to something deep within me. Even I used to believe this at one point. But that was as a child. Thankfully, years of stabilisers had talked sense into me. Stabilisers…yes…it had been more than two weeks since I had taken a dose. I needed to take a pill tonight.

Suddenly, the intercom buzzed and snapped me out of ADAM's head. I quickly hid his diary in a bathroom cabinet behind unopened bottles of shampoos and soaps, went into the living room and buzzed Caleb in. As he was making his way up to the eleventh floor, I threw my clothes in a laundry basket and scanned the area to get rid of anything conspicuous.

"I was starving. Figured you wouldn't have eaten either. So picked up a pizza." Caleb entered the apartment with a delicious aroma of roasted vegetables simmering under macadamia cheese. He was still in his work attire and looked drained from the day.

I set the dining table with two plates and a glass each for some red wine. He lifted the lid of the large cardboard box. Mitten, who had been napping peacefully after her dinner, sniffed the air and ran towards us. I looked into her eyes and was stern. "No Mit Mit. You've already eaten tonight." She actually listened and leapt back on the top seat of her scratching post.

The thin-crusted dough layered with capsicum,

olives, mushrooms, jalapenos, pineapples and roasted cashews, and topped with caramelised macadamia cheese turned my mild appetite into an insatiable hunger. I took one bite and almost forgot why Caleb was even here. A hot shower and a warm meal can do wonders for…the fabled soul.

"I expected you to be a mess." Caleb brought me back to reality before he bit into his slice. I was relieved he could not see any trace of the last few hours.

I was selective with my words but in essence told him about RYAN and how his body had turned up with multiple stabbing wounds in his stomach not long after I had last seen him alive. I reminded him of my own 'punch' from that night and floated the possibility of what if it was a premonition of the stabbing that led to his death. I looked at the floor while relaying this so as to not get intimidated by his expressions.

When I finished, I looked up. Caleb had stopped eating. His eyes had turned to stone. His face had lost all colour.

After what seemed like hours, his voice let out a restrained whisper. "It was *you* in that grainy footage?"

I nodded.

He sighed. "Is that all or is there more?"

I was tempted to tell him about the silicon microchip barcode RYAN had handed me. But something told to hold back. All I could say was, "I have a meeting with the Crime Branch tomorrow."

He jumped out of his chair as if it had been set on fire! "How did you even get into this mess? Ok Caleb…think…think…!" He charged from one end of the living room to another, and then back again. "Can you promise me just this one thing? Don't say anything that'll make *you* look crazy or get *you* in trouble! In fact, make it sound like you spoke to that guy for all of two seconds and hardly remember anything."

I saw the sense in his advice.

"You really need to focus on the nanochip and forget about everything else. Speaking of, please tell me you're back on stabilisers...?"

I could not tell him the truth, not now anyway. And I certainly could not tell him about my evening in ADAM's burnt apartment and the *click*.

"You need to be on stabilisers if you're speaking to the Crime Branch tomorrow!" His frustrated, steely eyes looked directly into mine.

"Of course, I'm back on them." I lied.

He did not seem convinced. Suddenly, he raced towards the door and said, "I've got to go. Just remembered something important."

After a few confused minutes, I got up and cleared the table. As I was preparing for bed, another notification popped up on my phone: *1 new email from the GridCare.*

GridCare was a universal healthcare insurance scheme that was funded by our taxes and operated by the Grid. What could they possibly want from me? It became clear after I opened the message.

Dear Ms Cassandra

Our records show you are three days overdue to refill your stabiliser prescription. To avoid any inconvenience to yourself or your employer, please have it filled immediately.

Also, please allow five minutes to help your pharmacist assess any implications from this delay.

Regards

GridCare

I kicked myself. How could I be so careless? The punishment for not fulfilling stabiliser prescriptions included heavy fines and even short jail sentences in some instances.

Tomorrow was going to be some day, first at the pharmacy and then at the Crime Branch. I took a stabiliser pill just before closing my eyes for the night. Outside, it snowed heavily. Inside, I slept like a brick in my warm bed surrounded by an eerie silence of never-ending darkness.

The next day, I got up early to go to my local pharmacy before work. My feet shuffled hurriedly over the sheets of crisp white snow. I cringed as soon as I entered the shopping mall. Flowers, hearts and teddy bears were everywhere. A Dean Martin song played in the background.

Let it snow, let it snow, let it snow!

Religions had faded but commercial holidays birthed by them were still going strong. Go figure!

By the time I got to the pharmacy, my annoyance was quite visible. However, it worked in my favour, for the pharmacist thought it was my disappointment in my own self for missing the refill. I played on that. It made my interview better than expected. Since I 'supposedly' had enough stabilisers to cover me for the next four days, the pharmacist deemed my offence to be excusable. He let me off with a warning. Also, he reminded me the GridCare mandated our prescriptions be filled by their due-date, which was set to a week before our pills ran out. Finally, he completed a form to have two points deducted from my HumanSite account.

I made a note to continue getting my refills on time, no matter what.

When I was back at work, I spent most of my morning in a *clean room*, which was a protected area that was heavily sterilized and where only a select few could enter. I busied myself with running assays on body samples of those who had experienced allergies to graphene in addition to silicon. One part of my brain was trying to understand what reactions were going on in people's bodies and how to best counter them. The other part was playing, *'let it snow, let it snow, let it snow!'*

A sharp voice broke my split thoughts. "Cassy darling, there you are! I have been looking all over."

Who the hell was Cassy?

EMMA knocked on the glass door. She was not in a protective gear and therefore, could not enter the room. I removed my lab coat and stepped out.

"I am organising a symposium. Humans plus Artificial Intelligence equals Infinite Potential. You better have the nanochip ready by then."

Before I could say yes or no, or ask for more information, she dashed off. I did not care. I looked up at the clock- 1330 hours. Something far more pressing was on my mind.

I signed out of the laboratory, picked up my coat and exited the Servitium building. I motioned to the nearest cab and set off to the Grid's headquarters.

The headquarters were hard to miss given they were situated in the most prominent building in the city. This building was a grey frame standing at almost two kilometres tall. One of its walls was green with the life of moss and other climber plants. This helped to reduce pollution levels and turn carbon dioxide into oxygen. Also, this absorbed sunlight, which insulated the building and maintained optimal temperatures inside.

Multiple foot-bridges and tunnels linked the headquarters to a few other buildings in the city. Most of the floors were restricted, requiring retina and fingerprint recognition. Also, there were rumours the building had ten additional floors underground, where only those with top-security clearance were allowed.

A Juli.R was stationed at the foyer reception and greeted me. "Good afternoon, Dr Rees. Agent JOHNSTON will be with you shortly."

I took a seat in the waiting area. The foyer was light and airy, and filled with beautiful plants. There was a palm-tree shaped fountain in a corner, which had water streaming out of its arms. Three large screens flashed details of meetings and events on common floors. A blue apparition floated in the corner. Wait…what? My neck spun to the right. RYAN was smiling with his bruised lips and broken teeth.

My eyes widened.

He waved and winked.

My jaw dropped.

"Dr Rees?" A voice called from behind. It was of a golden-haired man of medium build in his early thirties. He was dressed in a sharp, grey suit.

"Agent JOHNSTON?" I turned around to greet him, then discretely turned my head back to the right. But RYAN had faded away.

He nodded. "Thanks for coming in. We will keep this short."

He escorted me into an express lift, waved his hand at the scanner and pressed 166. We were immediately sucked up. Within seconds, doors opened to reveal a blue-grey ocean as far as I could see. He led me to a small room with a round table and three chairs. "This way please. My partner special agent FIELD will be joining us."

A tall, olive-skinned woman with short, brown hair entered. She seemed to be in her late twenties and was dressed in just as much grey as Agent JOHNSTON was.

"We will be recording this interview. We will also take notes." He looked up and scanned my face intently.

Could he read my guilt? I nodded cautiously in acknowledgement.

"Did you know MR RYAN ANGELO?" Agent FIELD commenced the session.

"Not personally." I replied.

"When did you last see him?" She continued.

Did five minutes ago count? Likely not.

"I only met him once- I was heading home after finishing work. He came out of nowhere and dragged me behind a tree. I thought I was being mugged!"

The Agent's eyes widened. "What else do you remember of that encounter?" She probed.

I tried my best to focus but Dean Martin's snow kept echoing in my mind. Somehow, I managed a response. "It lasted all of two seconds. I screamed. He ran away. Next thing, he turned up dead somewhere."

"What did he say to you?" Agent JOHNSTON asked.

Caleb's words echoed in my mind. 'Don't say anything that'll make *you* look crazy or get *you* in trouble!' I took a breath and was about to open my mouth when, to my absolute shock, an invisible hand poked me! I struggled to sit still. My eyes watered. Were my mental faculties declining and making me lose connection to reality?

Agent FIELD gave me a cold stare. I wiped my tears. "He didn't say anything. I was scared for my life. Like I said, I screamed. He ran away."

The agents looked at each other. Had I managed to convince them? Sorry RYAN for sullying your name. But this was the only way to steer them away from your piece of paper.

"We did a background check on you. So, you are a scientist at Servitium? Beauty and brains both." Agent JOHNSTON's voice was low and deep.

Before I could be lured into a false sense of security, Agent FIELD raised hers. "But we have an alert. You missed refilling your stabiliser prescription and had two points deducted from your HumanSite account this morning."

I was ready for this. I looked at Agent JOHNSTON and did my best damsel-in-distress impersonation. "Yes officers, this was totally my fault! I'm working day and night on the new chip. I was even awarded ten points on the HumanSite for my hard work recently. Since I still have enough pills to cover me, I thought to get my prescription filled on my day off. But after GridCare alerted me last night, I saw a pharmacist this very morning and here is my refill." I rummaged through my cluttered handbag and produced a small, glass bottle.

They both took notes.

Agent FIELD sniggered when asking the next question. "Did you know MR ADAM RODGER?"

Those investigators were indeed thorough. Then again, so was I. I straightened my shoulders confidently. "Only from the news. But yes, being a scientist, I became curious about him as a subject. I wanted to understand what drove him to his act of suicide and if his silicon microchip contributed to it. I need to make sure there's no such glitch in my nanochip."

"Does that to your mind justify breaking and entering?" Agent FIELD asked.

My heart raced frantically. I tried my best to keep a calm exterior.

"I apologise. Getting permissions takes time. There's a significant amount of pressure on me right now. We need to be on track to get hundred percent of the world's population nano-chipped in the next two years. I could not afford to deal with red tape at this time." It was amazing how much confidence I exuded once I put my scientific cap on.

"Bloody, arrogant scientists. Thinking they are above the law!" Agent FIELD hissed.

"The Grid has invested a lot in you. It wants to help you. We cannot have one of us running rogue and getting points deducted from the HumanSite." Agent JOHNSTON was more empathetic.

I switched back to my damsel-in-distress mode. "I understand. If I can share in confidence…I'm in the running for the Forcas Award this year. I don't want anything to sabotage it."

Both of the agents looked at each other. Agent JOHNSTON said, "Will you excuse us for a moment?" They left the room. When they came back, he said, "We suspect you have a personal connection to MR ADAM RODGER. We will not report your break-in because we recognise your contribution to our society.'

Agent FIELD was unnecessarily rude. "Consider this your first and final warning."

Before I could say anything to defend myself against the false accusation, Agent JOHNSTON repeated some of Caleb's words. "Please maintain your focus on the nanochip only. If you require assistance, please contact the appropriate branch." He escorted me out of the room and back into the main foyer. "We have high hopes from you, Cassandra," he said as we parted ways.

Their good cop bad cop routine left me with a migraine. I bought some fresh orange juice on my way back to the lab.

At 1800 hours, Dean Martin finally left me. As I was packing up to go home, a notification popped up from my personal account: *1 new email from Karon.*

Who was Karon?

When I clicked on the message below, it became clear.

Dear Cassandra

It will be my pleasure to talk to you about the nutritional benefits of bananas and beans. I will be at the New Green Centre 224 at 1:30 pm this Saturday. If you are still interested, please turn up.

Best wishes, Karon

Chapter 6 – The Lovers

If you are still interested, please turn up.

I stared at this message from Karon. Thankfully, Agent JOHNSTON's words talked sense into me. 'Please maintain your focus on the nanochip only...We have high hopes from you.' I listened to him, ignored the message and went home.

After a quick shower, I heated a bowl of homely pumpkin soup and toasted two freshly baked sourdough slices. I had dinner on the couch and streamed a *Real Housewives* episode in which one of the women had thrown a party. Everyone had gotten drunk and was spilling beans. Soon, it became a downward spiral of who had slept with whom, who had offered bribes to get their ratings up on HumanSite and who was not allowed to have a baby. Could you imagine me having a glass of wine with these lovely ladies? "Cassandra has been hallucinating! She says she had a premonition of RYAN ANGELO's murder! She broke into a dead man's apartment and stole his diary!" Now that would make for some dream ratings, no pun intended.

Mitten showed more sophistication and ignored those high-pitched voices. Instead, she stood up with a stiff tail and let out a low growl. To my surprise, she leapt onto Avantika.R and toppled it over! Was that simply her predator instinct or had her cute, little brain figured out it was a robot and not her sister?

My eyes were on the cat-robot mayhem when my phone buzzed. Caleb checked in about the Crime Branch: *How did it go?*

I messaged back: *Okay. I'll mind my own business from now on.*

He replied: *Sounds good! Up for some dessert?*

It was 2130 hours. A midnight blanket had layered the leftover sheet of snow. I did not want to leave Mitten alone after dark. But it had been more than a week since a shadow had last appeared. Our nights were slowly returning to normal. Maybe I could leave the lights on and go out for a quick hour…?

I wrote back: *Sure.*

He messaged: *I'll call a cab. See you outside yours in ten minutes.*

I changed out of my pyjamas and into a pair of dark blue jeans and a mauve top. I brushed my hair to make it neat and rubbed a serum all over to make it shine. After a thin coat of pink lip gloss, I grabbed a turquoise-coloured scarf and grey coat, and gave Mitten an air-kiss. I left a few lights on and went downstairs.

Caleb was waiting outside. The freezing wind bit me before I was in warmth of the cab with him.

"Wow! You made an effort for me." He teased.

I rolled my eyes. We both laughed.

"What brings you to my neighbourhood?" I asked.

"I felt guilty for running out on you last night. And I wanted to hear about the Crime Branch. But most importantly, I'm craving waffles of Mango Moksha."

"Yeah, about last night…everything okay?"

"All good. Just had to take care of something at work."

"Found aliens somewhere?"

"Not even one."

We laughed.

"By the way, Mango Moksha will be a nightmare tonight coz of lovebirds everywhere." I sighed.

"My cravings don't care." He replied.

Two minutes later, the cab dropped us outside the café's double-glass doors which had crimson hearts plastered all over. As soon as we walked in, my ears were confronted with even more cheesy love songs. Spiced chocolates and sweet fruits dominated the air inside. To top it all off, a Juli.R was at the counter giving everyone a forced smile.

When our turn came, we placed an order of Belgium waffles with strawberries and cream, a raw peanut butter cheesecake slice, a turmeric latte and a hot chocolate.

"Enjoy," the robot said with cold, creepy eyes.

"Is it plotting to kill us?" Caleb whispered after we walked away.

"Probably." I half-joked.

We found a quiet corner on that overflowing night where mythical love was on display in groups of two, three, four or more. Okay, so it was not really love; it was more lust and fetish. But at least the Valentine's Day had seers and organics celebrating under the same roof. Heck, some had even brought their robot companions out on a date as if it could eat something or feel anything!

I knew I loved you before I met you

I've been here waiting all my life.

Savage Garden, a band from the 1990s was blasting. Caleb took off his charcoal coat to reveal a crisp, ivory shirt with an Armani logo. Everyone around was equally matched in neutrals and pastels of designer wear. A number of faces were covered in three inches of makeup. Some perfumes had even fought hard with flavours of the café and made their way around. I felt so…underdressed.

PAULA brought our order. We repeated *smile and click*.

I scooped a piece of crunchy peanut, cashew cream and biscuit base with a fork. The hint of lemon in cashews brought out the pinch of salt in peanuts and balanced the overall sweetness perfectly.

Caleb was already half-way through his first waffle.

"That good, huh?" I smiled.

He nodded with a full mouth and offered me a square. The crispy piece turned soft and fluffy in my mouth after just one bite.

"We should do this more often." He suggested as he dug into my cheesecake.

"Sounds like a plan." I replied, for who in their right mind would say no to delicious dessert?

Massacred, velvet roses were displayed on every table, including ours. Tea-light candles were burning for us. Even the sky outside showered snowflakes to match the rhythm of legendary Beatles.

Something in the way she moves
attracts me like no other lover.

Could this setting be any more awkward?

To normalise the evening, I blurted. "I need to present at a symposium but have no idea what to say!"

"Ah...you'll be fine." Caleb ran his fingers through his curly, dark hair.

After a few minutes, I got up and walked to the counter to get some water for the table. When I was heading back with a jug and two empty glasses, a short, dark-haired woman bumped into me. The impact splashed some of the water onto my clothes.

"Gotchya!" The woman laughed. Her dark, beady eyes looked me up and down.

My sinking feeling returned. "Next time, watch where you walk." I gritted my teeth.

PAULA rushed over, took the jugs and glasses from my hands and put them on an empty table nearby. She handed me some napkins. While I dried myself, she wiped the floor.

"Sorry! Was only joking." CHANDRIANA replied coarsely. Her mouth ripped open into a malicious smile and revealed sharp canines.

I groaned.

She shrugged her shoulders and walked away.

CHANDRIANA repulsed me. I would have already kicked her off my study if my hands were not ticd.

"Everything okay?" Caleb asked when I was back on our table.

"Argh! That creepy woman's in my study. I have a feeling she's out to get me."

"Maybe it was just an accident…?"

"Maybe..."

PAULA brought fresh water to us. I looked over to CHANDRIANA, who was seated a few tables away. Her eyes were fixed on me while her male companion talked to her.

"Did you see the news today?" Caleb changed

the subject.

"No. Why?" I looked at him and forced a smile.

"That Rebellion group I told you about…it's gaining momentum. First, it was just isolated protests. But now, new chapters are opening all over."

"What a waste of time." I sipped turmeric latte; its earthiness was a compliment to my creamy dessert and eased my nerves.

"The Grid's gonna come down hard on whoever joins them. It's best for us to stay away." Caleb sipped his hot chocolate.

"Of course." I could not believe even I was questioning the Grid just a few days ago! I *had* to throw ADAM's diary away and forget about RYAN.

"And…just be careful. You're on the Grid's radar now. They may be keeping a close eye on you."

I flinched.

We finished our drinks and dessert in silence. Caleb settled the bill despite my insistence to pay for my half. As we were exiting the café, I looked over my shoulder. CHANDRIANA was still in her seat, this time talking to her companion.

Caleb dropped me outside my building. We kissed goodbye.

I went up to my apartment and opened the door. Complete darkness confronted me as soon as I walked in. This was strange because…had I not left the lights on..?

"Mitten!" I called out.

No response.

"Mitten!" I tried again, this time with a sinking stomach.

Once again, no response.

My mind flashed back to the evening from a few weeks ago when I had gotten lost in Rheedum and come home late. My already unsettled gut became clenched. I ran to the nearest switch. Just as I was about to flick it, I tripped on something and fell to the floor. An icy cold and a sickly-sweet air hit my nose. I quickly got up. A cold draft brushed across my body. Mitten hissed and jumped in front of me.

I lost all senses and collapsed! Dare I say, I entered a dream-like state in which I was floating in a vacuum. Something invisible was sucking my lifeforce away and trying to drag me down into a black hole.

I fought back with all my strength.

I do not know how long this limbo lasted for. However, just as my depleted self was about to give up, my phone rang loudly. The sharp tone jolted me out of my trance. I woke up with a splitting headache.

"Cassandra! Can you start early today? We've got unexpected visitors arriving in just under an hour." Ellie, the human half of PROF AMON's two assistants, cried at the other end.

The room was still spinning. "What time is it?" I mumbled.

"Seven. You don't sound well. Everything okay?"

Gosh! How long had I been out for?

"I feel sick!" I yelped.

I looked around. Mitten was by my feet licking herself.

"Can you come in for a couple of hours? Please? The Dream Catcher team wasn't due until next week. But their chief executive was called to Geneva and leaves today. DAVE really wants you here to talk about the chip," Ellie said in one long breath.

I scanned my home. Everything was practically untouched. Everything except for…three dining table chairs that were toppled over.

What exactly had happened last night?

"Please?" Ellie repeated.

"I…I need to…. I'll be there at eight thirty for an hour." I hung up.

I went to the bedroom and stood in front of the full-length mirror to check my body for cuts, bruises and swelling. There were none. But a voice was screaming cruel words in my mind. "You are worthless! You deserve to die!" This, oddly, unsettled me even more. What had broken into my home, lurked in darkness, attacked me as soon as I came back and left me unconscious?

I opened a can of tuna. Mitten came running and devoured it. I went to the bathroom and pulled ADAM's diary out. The tornado of my hands tore some pages when turning them. I stopped at a note half-way through. It read: *Dreaming is the essence of our soul. It connects us to our past, our roots, our intuition, the Universe. Without dreaming, our soul has no voice. But, where does a dream end and a hallucination begin? What if the two are the same, except that one is with eyes closed and the other with eyes wide open? And it is us humans who do not understand, therefore, we do not know how to react!*

My fingers tapped restlessly on the diary. Where had I read this before? I bit into my nails and walked up and down my living room. Where….? Think Cassandra! Where….?

Finally, I remembered! I logged onto my blog: My adventures in Andromeda. I searched for a comment someone had left a while back. My impatient fingers scrolled the screen of my phone until it came to a short story I had written weeks ago. One of my few active followers, R0DG3R5, had made a post under it. His last actually. It was exactly the same as what was written in ADAM's diary!

Dreaming is the essence of our soul. It connects us to our past, our roots, our intuition, the Universe. Without dreaming, our soul has no voice. But, where does a dream end and a hallucination begin? What if the two are the same, except that one is with eyes closed and the other with eyes wide open? And it is us humans who do not understand, therefore, we do not know how to react!

I searched for the remaining comments R0DG3R5 had left on my blog. Two in particular caught my eyes. The first read: *We need to meet soon. Time is running out for the both of us!*

My legs turned to noodles. My cloudy head hung low.

The second read: *I'm finally going to escape.*

NewsLink had reported these were ADAM's words just before he jumped off the City Bridge! Was R0DG3R5 actually ADAM RODGERS? Was this why the investigators had said, 'We suspect you have a personal connection to MR ADAM RODGERS?'

Pins and needles travelled through my body. My jittery hands continued to turn pages to find clues in ADAM's thoughts.

Another phrase read: *I am seeing them everywhere. I hope the Dreaming group can help.*

The Dreaming group?! I immediately pulled out Karon's email. The same email I had ignored earlier. My shaking fingers typed: *Thanks for getting back to me. Can we meet sooner please? Like today?*

After sending the message, I took a deep breath and brushed my teeth. It was already 0750 hours. I had a quick shower and got dressed in a figure-hugging grey dress. I packed some of Mitten's treats and dry biscuits, and knocked on Richard's door.

"Everything all right, kiddo?" He yawned.

"I need a favour. Can you please look after Mitten until I get back? I'll explain later, I promise." I quivered.

He narrowed his eyes and opened his mouth to say something but refrained at the last second. Instead, he smiled and said, "Anything for you and the fluffy."

I took a deep breath and stepped out to face the day.

It was only a few more hours until another night. Whether this was all in my head or out there in the real world, it was gaining momentum. The clock was ticking. My clock…

Fifteen minutes later, I arrived at work. Ellie showed me the room in which the meeting was being held. It had only just begun. Key members attending from our side included Sara and NIKKI, and of course EMMA, who was hunched in a corner.

From the Dream Catcher team, there were two attendees. The first was the chief executive DR DEE HEATH, who was six foot tall and in her late fourties. She wore a black business suit and thick glasses. Her auburn hair was pulled back in a tight ponytail, revealing every single freckle on her forehead. The second was Dr Steven Wilson, a neurosurgeon who was five feet ten and in his late twenties. He wore a navy business suit that complimented his sandy brown hair and blue-green eyes.

PROF DAVE AMON was at the head of the table. He was dressed in a designer black suit, underneath which was a crisp red shirt and a silk, white tie.

I sat next to Sara. After brief introductions, DR HEATH commenced her presentation. "Dreams are unstable. They replay our painful memories and make us depressed. They conjure up monsters and give us a fright. What if we let machines sift through this junk in our mind and pass on only better, more stable dreams to us?"

What a strong and timely opening! I was keen to see where it was going and if there was any weight to rumours of mind control.

"To achieve this, we built on the famous Dream Catcher project, which studied brain activity with MRI and decoded dreams into images. We developed an algorithm to predict which emotion each of these images will generate. We uploaded approved images that invoked favourable emotions onto our software to create random sequences. These sequences are what we call the AI dreams. We only catalogue dreams that result in at least ninety percent pleasant emotions." She continued.

"What is the benefit?" PROF AMON asked.

DR HEATH handed over to Dr Wilson to continue. "This will allow us to, before we fall asleep, choose which of the catalogued dreams we want to play overnight. It is no secret when we access pleasant emotions during sleep, we wake up feeling good the next day. AI dreams can, at an individual level, improve our ability to learn and produce. On a collective level, they can lead to a happier world."

"Sure. But we're doing just fine without dreams. What's the need now?" I probed.

"The real need is for the second phase. If this

first phase works out, we plan to format skills such as mathematics, languages and sciences in a dream sequence. People can 'download' these while they sleep and wake up smarter the next day."

"You mean…have computer-like upgrades and downloads?" Sara asked.

Dr Wilson nodded.

So this was where rumours of mind control came from! Although…if executed ethically, imagine how this could enhance our abilities. After-all, peer-reviewed research has already demonstrated when we listen to something while falling asleep, it connects with our subconscious mind, and we understand and retain it better. Then why not take this next step?

"Neo from Matrix, anyone?" NIKKI said.

Everyone laughed.

DR HEATH continued. "What we need is the right chip that will support this functionality."

"And this is where our nano comes in!" PROF AMON exclaimed.

My phone flashed a notification: *1 new email from Karon*. It read: *Sure, I can meet any time after 11 am today at the New Green Centre 224.*

I quickly typed back: *See you at 1100 hours then!*

EMMA cleared her throat and gave me a stern look. Everyone else in the room was too hypnotised to notice my brief moment of distraction.

"Can this really help us to have better dreams?" Sara asked.

"Absolutely! In theory, our entire brain is active when we dream. But certain parts such as the pineal gland are unstable and best not encouraged. This does not mean we have to miss out on the function they were supposed to serve." DR HEATH replied.

Pineal gland. I had not heard anyone mention it before. I made a note to look it up.

"The silicon microchip is not compatible with the bandwidth we use. This is why we are interested in your nano," Dr Wilson said.

I had no idea this body of work was happening behind the scenes. A part of me was excited, although an even bigger part was cautious.

PROF AMON replied. "Our partnership can certainly revolutionise the human experience. Cassandra is leading development of the graphene nanochip. Cassandra, will you give us an overview?"

I smiled and commenced my talk. "It is no secret microchips help us to integrate with AI better. However, for many like me, our own physiology has been a roadblock, where these cause anaphylactic reactions. My solution is the next generation chip, a nano, which is one billionth fraction of a unit. Being significantly smaller than a microchip, it has the ability to embed within us at a deeper level and live in our body as our own. Made of graphene, it will be a faster and a better conductor than anything we have seen before. Our last three clinical trials have already shown promising results. We are waiting on results from seven more before moving to the next phase."

"Impressive! We are in the final stages of our last two trials with the silicon. It has been a tremendous opportunity to learn from our subjects. Steven is wrapping this up for me while I am away. Hopefully our next set of trials will be with the nano," DR HEATH said.

PROF AMON had a big smile. His chest was puffed out.

More discussion followed, after which PROF

AMON said, "I will talk to my lawyers and draw up a contract. Cassandra will be the contact from our end."

DR HEATH replied. "Steven will be ours. Well, we better get going. It is almost time for my flight."

The meeting finished on time. As we were packing up, DR HEATH said to Dr Wilson, "Let me know if you have any issue accessing the Global Microchip Database in my absence."

My ears perked up. My body froze. Was this the same Global Microchip Database that contained details of who was allocated what barcode on Earth?!?

I looked straight into their eyes with shock. They looked back into mine with confusion.

Chapter 7 – The Chariot

"The cab will be here any minute." Ellie popped her head through the door.

I cleared my throat and said, "Thanks Ellie; I was just going to ask DR HEATH and Dr Wilson if they wanted me to order one."

DR HEATH thanked us and finished packing up. PROF AMON and I accompanied her and Dr Wilson to the ground floor. As soon as they got into their cab, I excused myself. PROF AMON went back to work while I walked to a nearby café for an almond cappuccino to go. The smooth sips warmed me as I made my way in melting snow to the New Green Centre 224, also known as NGC 224.

NGC 224 was a colourful oasis in the middle of a concrete urban desert that was our city. It was surrounded by office and residential high-rise buildings that spanned more than two kilometres in height on all four sides. It had benches and manicured areas for those who wanted to sit; and jogging tracks for those who wanted to run. Some parts were protected, as in, we could not go there because the council was growing flowers such as orange witch hazel, pink winter cherry, purple pansies and red cyclamen. Together, their fragrances made the crisp winter air also sweet and delicious.

I followed a path that led me to a small pond,

the centre of which was a tall statue of a woman leaning against a rock. She was holding a vessel through which water was flowing; its streams were dancing in striking swirls and stunning spirals. Bright blue and pale green birds were chirping in harmony with these splashes.

This was rare because by 2061, seventy percent of the Earth was either burnt or barren. Outside of urban settlements, there were minimal infrastructures or natural resources to support us. Contamination of land was so significant and quality of air was so low we would not survive. Then again, the urban land we were living on was barely keeping us happy and the urban air we were breathing was only just keeping us alive. Therefore, an oasis such as this was both a blessing and a responsibility. I made a note to come here more and spend time in the company of soft, serene nature.

While I was lost in my thoughts, someone tapped on my shoulder. I turned around and met the electric blue eyes of a smiling five foot one blond who had purple highlights. She was in her late thirties, and wore a red coat and a matching scarf.

"Cassandra? Hi, it's Karon. Sorry, I searched online to see what you looked like."

She seemed normal enough. Still, I maintained my caution. "Bananas and beans, huh?" I asked after brief introductions.

She laughed. "It's our code coz to an outsider, it sounds silly. But these are, in fact, foods of a dreamer. Cheap and readily available."

I shot her a blank stare.

"Bananas and beans contain a lot of nutrition, especially vitamin B6 and amino acid tryptophan. We need these to create serotonin in our bodies, which keeps our brain alert during sleep and gives us our dreams." She explained in a language I understood.

I could not believe we were actually talking about nutritional benefits of bananas and beans!

"But aren't dreams a mental disorder?" I asked.

"Quite the contrary! Dreams are a combination of our thoughts, visions and sensations. Some are vivid, as in, they feel intense and life-like. Others are even lucid, as in, we can control them to gain experiences and access knowledge of our choosing. If exercised correctly, dreams can make us a better version of ourselves." Her words floated out like poetry.

"Even when they're filled with nightmares?" I asked.

She nodded. "Especially when they're filled with nightmares! Coz that's our subconscious telling us what we need to work on."

This Dreaming group came across as an assembly of pseudo-scientists who were running a self-improvement experiment based on nutrition science. What would they think about Dr Wilson's Dream Catcher project...?

"How did you find us anyway?" Karon asked.

I relayed the evening from almost two months ago when a big gush of wind blew the flyer straight into my lap. I was clear it was not my fault and that it just happened.

"Would you believe whoever finds us does so under the most unusual of circumstances...like it's fated!"

"Really?"

Karon nodded. "The Universe broadcasted this group to me loud and clear through a series of events. Other members describe similar experiences too."

I did not believe in fate, therefore, redirected the conversation to something more tangible. "How many members are in your group?"

"Seven. I'm the scout. I use my intuition to suss out all newbies before letting them in. We don't want the Grid infiltrating us."

My mind drifted off to ADAM and RYAN.

"Well… there were more. But their journey was cut short due to…mishaps." Karon continued as if she had read my thoughts.

"I'm sorry to hear this," I said.

Lunchtime crowd was building up in the park. Our quiet corner soon became a hot-spot for those who wanted to soak up the sun. Karon and I moved to a bench that was under shade. Once we were seated, my mind went straight to ticking off questions from my list.

"How about the news lately? People are hallucinating and killing themselves!"

Karon's face turned solemn. She interrogated my eyes. "You're seeing shadows too?"

"N-no!" I stammered.

She leaned in closer. "It's okay if you are. When we stop taking stabilisers, we start to see the world as it really is. Totally worth the two points you lost on HumanSite."

"H-how do you know?"

"I'm the scout, remember."

Her directness pierced through my defences. "Not that I've seen any…but…but what exactly are these shadows anyway?" I asked after a moment's hesitation.

She sighed. "Minions. Bottom-feeders who do

dirty work for Demiurge, or as some may say, the Devil-god. They appear scary but are actually quite weak."

"The Devil-god? Isn't this a myth!"

"That it's a myth is the ultimate trick! Religions all over the world have fought since conception but have agreed on this one thing. That our soul, which is our ultimate essence, is priceless. Sacred texts have documented we must save our soul, the battle is for our soul, the devil wants our soul, and so forth." Karon's voice became lower and faster.

What had I gotten myself into? Was this Dreaming group a cult?

"The only way to fight these minions is to fully wake our soul up. Our group's trying to figure out how. Some members have even taken psychedelics, actually no, plant medicines like N,N Dimethyltryptamine and Caapi. These shut down the fear part of our mind and let our soul speak."

"N-N what?"

"DMT." She chuckled.

Psychedelics were controversial. Most were banned and called for severe penalties. Talking about them, the Devil and soul left me unsettled. Karon seemed nice enough. But this was a mistake.

I got up to leave.

She grabbed my arm and prompted me to run. I stumbled. We took our shoes off. She held my hand in hers. We picked up speed with our bare feet. Gosh, we did a lap of the whole park in seven minutes! By the time we stopped, I was puffing and panting. Karon, on the other hand, stretched her arms and legs as if she was ready for more.

"I suppose it's a good idea to get my fitness up

so I can run the next time I see a minion," I said between breaths, and pictured myself grabbing Mitten and dashing to the door.

"Not to run from, silly! Exercise, especially with bare feet, helps us to ground. It makes us feel our body and develop a strong connection with it."

"To ground means to be in the here and the now, right?" I quoted from a new-age article I had read months ago.

"Ha! Sure!"

I was confused.

"A better meaning of grounding is to see the truth without wavering or falling apart. To see things as they really are without our mind fleeing into denial. We can do this only if we're strong. And this strength comes only if our physical and spiritual selves, or our body and soul, are connected. Without this, we're at mercy of our mind, which is notorious for turning us into self-absorbed pieces of mess."

This was an unusual explanation. "Okaaayyy... so what's the easiest way to have this connection?" I asked.

"Firstly, we must show respect towards our body and protect it from harm."

Finally! Something that made sense. Maybe I could stay for a few more minutes.

Just then, a sparrow flew past us. Karon said, "See that bird? Maybe it has somewhere important to go. Then again, maybe not. The main thing is, it can fly and so it does. Do we understand our capabilities like a bird does its? Or are we living in amnesia?"

I was a scientist. Still, my knowledge had gaps about human anatomy, physiology and biochemistry. Who would have thought the first lesson on dreaming was to connect with our physical body, the same body we reject to follow our dreams!

We took our coats off and walked back to the bench. Karon was wearing a heart-shaped transparent locket that contained some resin, a few metal shavings and a clear stone. Where had I seen this before?

"Argonite. It's good for health and wellbeing. You should get one too," she said when she saw me staring.

I nodded as if I understood.

Karon told me she used to be a nurse but was now an artist. That she was once a fellow health professional eased me. Also, she had spent time in a remote monastery years ago. It all began when she announced her sexuality to her conservative parents with hope for support. Instead, she was met with disdain in which they disowned her because her choices did not fit in with the Grid's plan for her life. Broken, she left their house. Through a series of events and kindness of strangers, she stumbled upon meditation, which eventually led her to one of the last monasteries remaining. There, she found peace and discovered dreaming.

Karon was in her early twenties and living halfway across the world when the ban first came about. I was a lost teenager who had just moved out of her parents' house.

"Stabilisers and technology. That's what the Grid used. Even I bought it for years." There was regret in her voice.

I did not know how to respond, therefore, strung some consolation words together. "Everyone did. Who wants a massive deduction from their HumanSite account and a prison sentence?"

"The law was the worst. It was made under the guise of uniting microchipped organics who could not dream anymore with seers who still could. But this disconnected us even more and turned us against each other." She recounted with a hint of pain.

This was the first time someone had openly spoken about the ban.

I leaned in and finally asked the main question I came for. "Did you know RYAN or ADAM?"

Her eyes narrowed. She paused, then said, "Drifters they were. And…they were convinced you'd join us one day."

"W-what?" I pulled back.

She looked around and cleared her throat. "They followed your work. But let's not talk about it here. Why don't you come to our meeting this Sunday?"

I wanted to keep my life separate from this mumbo-jumbo. I wanted to close this eccentric chapter altogether. I did not want to join a Dreaming group and encourage it!

Karon noticed my hesitation. I felt guilty and took details out of politeness.

We put our shoes and coats back on. As we were parting ways, she said, "If you see another minion, 'will' yourself. If you're clear, nothing will stand in your way."

"Huh?" I really was coming across quite dumb in this conversation. Maybe it was a good thing…?

She made slow and focused movements with her arms and legs as if spelling something. 'Our free-will, which is our ability to choose freely, is the ultimate tool we have. It can even change the course of tide and move mountains. Therefore, if another shadow bothers you, shine light on it and say out loud, I will myself to be safe and protected."

Sounded simple enough. But was it really? Had I not tried this last night? But instead of retreating, that shadow had scraped my wound and used my pain against me! I told this to Karon. She asked, "Did you will yourself? Did you own your space?"

Mitten did. But did I?

"These minions have been stalking us, leeching off our soul for millenniums. Off every single human in the world!" There was anger in her voice.

"Even organics? They don't have a soul…not that I believe in one anyway."

"Says who? Technology has crippled us, regardless of whether we're seers or organics. We've lost our will, our patience, our intrinsic 'why.' As in, why are we here and what is the purpose of our life? If an organic finds their will and why, they find their soul. On the other hand, if we the seers lose our will and why, we also lose our soul."

This challenged my simplistic understanding of organics and seers. The understanding that was fed to me by the Grid in which organics were superhumans and seers were primitives waiting for an upgrade. I felt the need to defend myself and said, "I know what my why is."

"Will yourself to remember it even more clearly so you can fulfil it the right way."

I thought of the chip and said, "I will myself to remember."

We continued on this topic for a few more minutes and counted all the possible whys we could think of. These are listed below:

- To advance technology for the greater good.
- To bring new knowledge in fields of science, medicine or mathematics.
- To share esoteric wisdom and alternate ways to heal.
- To expand creativity in arts, music and other forms of expression.
- To conserve environment and natural resources.
- To advocate for those, including other life forms, who cannot stand up for themselves.
- To take care of someone who has something important to learn or a valuable purpose to fulfil.
- To help others as and when they need us.

Some of these whys sound more glamourous than others. But no one why is any less or more important than any other. Also, our why may change depending on where we are in our life. As long as we do our part to keep our planet spinning.

What part are *you* playing?

While we were talking, the sun started to fade. "Another long night coming up!" I sighed.

"One more of many." Karon sighed back.

We parted ways.

What an unlikely connection this was. And to think it was born out of a coincidence that was a gush of wind. Or...dare I ask...was it the hand of fate? Regardless, I felt even more obliged to get to the bottom of INC0418402. Would it be all right if I struck a friendship with Steven, who was on a completely opposite path to the Dreaming group, so he would allow me access to the Global Microchip Database?

I walked home while reflecting on the recent events. That a Demiurge was sending his minions to drain us was too far-fetched. I was not going to get carried away by such fear-based emotions. But I did agree we needed to take charge of our life-force, regardless of whether machines were in the equation or not. Because yes, scientifically we could get chipped and merge with AI, and become superhumans. However, if we were not careful, we could also become empty shells of our real selves.

We were still an hour away from the complete cover of dark. Mitten had been waiting at Richard's. I brought her home and gave her kisses. She got annoyed and struggled to free herself. I laughed and put her down on the floor. She ran away and played in a corner.

The nature of reality was unfolding before my eyes. What if, instead of denying it or getting scared, I paid attention and learnt?

As a first step, I had to prepare for tonight and any minion that turned up.

Chapter 8 – The Strength

How does one protect themselves from minions that hide in the dark and manipulate one's emotions?

To find an answer, I opened my laptop and typed, *'minions of Demiurge.'* Surprise, surprise, the search showed no results. I became creative with my keywords and looked for *'shadows that leech off humans.'* Pages upon pages of medical information on how to get rid of leeches and parasites came up. Also, there were blogs where writers had ranted about their leeching family and friends. I got sucked into juicy dramas of strangers, and before I knew, one click led to another and I was watching a video of a cat barking at a dog! Two whole hours had gone by.

Mitten slept next to me that whole time. Seeing her heavy eyes made me want to doze off as well. But I needed to maintain focus. I went to my bathroom and pulled ADAM's diary out from behind shampoo and soap bottles. I returned to my bed and played a meditation track in which a woman chanted "AUM" to sounds of Tibetan bowls. In this ethereal setting, I opened ADAM's diary.

The first page had familiar letters: *DREAMS.*

I turned over to the next page, which read: *Nothing has been the same since I lost JOSIE. She was only five. ANDREA never saw her gentleness the way I did. To her, she was trouble. To me, she needed love.*

Heaviness entered my heart. I continued to read.

I remember the calm Wednesday morning when my little girl was born. She weighed less than a feather. We did not expect her to survive. The hospital kept her for monitoring until she learnt to breathe. ANDREA gave up on her; she even gave up on us. But I could not. Like my little girl, I fought hard. Soon, we were a family. Or...was that all in my head? For ANDREA never stayed home with us. She found JOSIE and her drawings creepy. So what if she drew shadows? 'Look at this! One head...two heads...three heads.....!' ANDREA would crumble the thin sheets and throw them all over the floor.

I could not read another word. I put the diary down and closed my eyes. Soon, a restless sleep came over.

I was floating in darkness when cold, lanky fingers tapped on my toes. I turned to my side and tucked my feet under the blanket. The tapping continued. I half-opened my eyes and, to my absolute horror, met the glowing, red balls of a tall, ghoulish shadow standing at the edge of my bed!

I screamed at the faceless humanoid and got up.

The air around me turned into icicles and pierced my bones. Heaviness crept up behind me. My heart leapt into my throat. I jumped off the bed. But my legs refused to carry my weight. I fell on the floor and struggled to pull air in.

A second later, everything disappeared. JOSIE's cries flooded my ears. They merged with my own from when I was ten years of age. I was locked up in a small, dark room because my parents wanted to "beat out my fear of dark." My eyes watered. I drowned deeper and deeper into the tears that flowed out.

Mitten, my familiar, let out distant screams. Her "meow, meow" broke my trance. Karon's voice echoed. "Will yourself!" My mind fought a losing battle against the past and yelled, "I will myself to be safe and protected. I will myself to be safe and protected." Before I knew, I was shouting this out loud.

The painful memories withdrew their grip. I collapsed on the floor and took my first breath in who knows how long.

Enough was enough! I was not a helpless child anymore. I needed to let this part of me go. The part that had scrambled my brain and turned me into a victim.

A storm had built outside. I got up with renewed determination and peeled the curtains. Nature was going to be raw soon. With Mitten in my arms, I witnessed every moment of it, for it matched what had woken up within me.

The next morning, Richard, Laura and I were having brunch at Mango Moksha. Its crimson hearts and bleeding roses were gone. The background music was back to an eclectic mix of life and its many challenges. The air was once again of cinnamon spices and ground coffee. And I was on my usual seat with almond cappuccino and smashed avocado on toasted sourdough slices.

Richard took a sip of his latte and pulled up the NewsLink site on his mobile phone.

Military captures rebels; interrogation underway

Yesterday evening, based on a citizen tip, military personnel raided an underground hide-out of the Rebellion group in Front Pier. Two males, aged 41 years and 23 years, and a female aged 32 years, were captured. The Crime Branch is interrogating them to determine identity and whereabouts of their leader.

This group was planning riots between organics and seers. Its demands include reclassifying a mental disorder as normal and having protective surveillance removed.

Doing so will compromise our safety and put everyone at risk.

Please contact the Grid's Crime Branch in confidence if you have any information.

"Poor buggers!" Richard sighed.

"Shhhh…..!" Laura nearly choked on her bite of a blueberry pancake.

"Are they right or misguided?" I asked.

"Of course, misguided!" She shot me a cold look.

"Are they really?" Richard snapped.

Laura's fork slipped out of her hands and landed on her plate, making a slight bell.

"Back in the day, even I protested against the ban. Bloody Grid took me as a prisoner and…." he said.

"Enough! We promised to never talk about this!" She cut him short.

That cosy brunch suddenly turned cold.

"Excuse me." Streams escaped Laura's eyes. She got up and scurried to the door.

"Sorry kiddo. We'll talk later." Richard ran after her.

Their half-finished burger and pancakes were left behind along with their half-full drinks. I sipped on my cappuccino and wondered what exactly had happened when the Grid had arrested Richard…

The next day, I made my way to my first formal meeting with the Dreaming group.

Temperature outside was close to freezing. Dark clouds had taken over the sky. Karon met me a few minutes away from the venue. We both hugged our coats tight as we walked to a terrace house on a leafy street.

When we arrived, Karon signalled me to switch off my phone. I was hesitant at first but when she turned hers off, I did the same. She buzzed the intercom. A tall man in his late fifties with a muscular built and peppery hair opened the door. He was wearing dark jeans and a pale blue tee-shirt.

"Welcome Cassandra! I'm Gabe Walton, the coordinator of our group." He introduced himself and collected our phones. "We always leave them downstairs in the designated area so the Grid doesn't overhear us." He explained and led us up to the attic.

It was toasty inside. We took our coats off. Karon was wearing a long, flowing orange dress. I was in dark blue jeans and a burgundy top.

"We meet here coz the attic's large enough to accommodate ten people and ordinary enough to not draw attention." Karon explained.

Gabe had set the space up as a home-gym to deflect any questions. "It forces me to exercise!" He flexed his muscles, and pointed at metallic dumbbells and rubber coated weights, which were stacked next to an electric treadmill.

"Karon tells me ADAM and RYAN were a part of this group too…?" I asked.

Gabe nodded. "RYAN attended a conference last year, where you spoke about the power of imagination and shared your fascination with Andromeda. He told ADAM and both started following not just your nanochip progress but also your blog."

"I'm sorry they're not here with us anymore," I said. I had no idea my ice breaker to calm my own nerves in front of a large audience had set this course in motion!

"ADAM's suicide was a shock to us. As for RYAN...well he was a drifter. Very intelligent but kept mostly to himself."

I was surprised to hear this. RYAN's social media profile showed him to be of an outgoing nature.

"I wish I'd made more effort." Gabe continued.

I thought about RYAN's cryptic note and ADAM'S diary. As tempted as I was to offload these burdens, I decided to wait until I knew Gabe better.

During our conversation, I found out Gabe was one of the last human radiologists before this role was fully assigned to machines in 2054. This was because machines could identify even the tiniest speck of growth with hundred percent accuracy, something a human could never do with even the best training and tools. He felt his entire life had been rendered meaningless. This sent him into a spiralling depression that lasted three years. One day, "something happened" and he said, "enough!" That was the day he decided on a new purpose and commenced his research into human mind and soul. Shortly after, he started the Dreaming group to bring like-minded people together.

"Can't believe it's coming up to two years!" Karon said.

"Time flies when you're having fun!" Gabe laughed.

Suddenly, there was a heavy pour outside. "This weather calls for pumpkin spice latte with biscuits." Karon went to the kitchenette and boiled some water. She opened a pack of ginger biscuits and a jar of latte mix. I pulled a few mugs and a carton of almond milk out from a small cupboard and laid them on the bench. Gabe arranged the corner-stacked chairs in a circle of eight. After he was done, he went downstairs and brought a bunch of bananas from the main kitchen.

Soon, five unfamiliar faces turned up. Greetings filled the room.

"You must be Cassandra," a friendly voice said.

I smiled and nodded at the six foot frame with blond hair and deep brown eyes.

"I'm Divine. Welcome."

Divine was a male transitioning into a female and had seen some rather dark days because of her struggles. One day, purely out of coincidence, she met Gabe, who offered her an understanding her own family could not. "After some very persistent signs, I joined the Dreaming group," she said.

The group's remaining four members were Michael, a twenty-eight-year-old who had medium height and dark hair; Hemmy, a twenty-six-year-old who was tall and had sandy hair; Vicki, a thirty-five-year-old who was a redhead of my height and JOEL BENSEN, a tall fourty-two-year-old with a shaved head.

After everyone introduced themselves to me, Gabe clapped his hands. "We'll be starting in two minutes. Please grab yourself a hot drink and some nibbles."

Everyone grabbed a banana, and filled their mugs with latte mix and hot water. Within seconds, aromas of cinnamon, nutmeg and cloves spread through the entire room. Karon passed around a tray of biscuits. When we dipped these in our mugs, ginger joined in as well. The ambiance became soft and mysterious, with candles flickering in every corner and dimly lit lamps casting long shadows on the walls.

Gabe played a calming track on a dated device. Within seconds, we were in a whispering forest where birds were chirping and water was flowing.

"My friend on the inside tells me there have been three more suicides coz of minions." Gabe opened the session.

"I don't remember reading about them!" I was startled.

"These deaths are being under-reported. So far, the real tally is thirty eight and not the official five." He replied.

"What?!" The room echoed. My own voice was in the mix too.

"How much can we trust your friend?" JOEL asked. He was a banker who had overdosed on drugs and alcohol when partying one weekend. He survived but his old self did not. Although he still held the same job, he could not go back to the same lifestyle and joined the group two months ago when the Dreaming flyer "found" him.

Gabe replied. "A lot."

"Are we next?" Divine asked. Everyone's expressions changed. It was as if she had said their worst fear out loud.

"Come to think of it, I haven't seen Cynthia in

the last couple of weeks," Vicki said. She had helped Gabe to set up this group. Also, they had dated briefly but remained friends when it did not work out.

"She disappears every now n then. Living on streets can't be easy. In all fairness, the Community Branch tried to rehome her a few times. But she kept running away," Karon said.

"Who is Cynthia?" I asked.

"She's another one that drifts in n out of our lives. She once had a promising career in finance. But it all became too much for her and she spiralled out of control." Karon replied.

"She has schizophrenia. It can be easily managed but she's suspicious of authorities." Gabe added.

"Well…I can relate to that!" Hemmy scoffed.

The room burst out into laughter.

Hemmy was Gabe's son. He became interested in dreams a year ago when he saw his father change the course of his life for the better.

What a pleasant surprise it was to finally see a healthy parent-offspring relationship! I thought these existed only in movies and books.

"She's scary, man! All she talks about is demons," Michael said. He was taking environmental studies at a local university and had found the group late one night after a far-out conversation with a stranger. That stranger was Hemmy.

I immediately flashed back to a few months ago when I was chased by a homeless lady who had screamed, "You n me, n we, n all are cursed; demons live inside us." I nervously shifted in my chair. "I think I've met her. She told me to run n hide coz demons were coming for me," I said.

"Yeah…that'll be her." Hemmy rolled his eyes.

Gabe's already solemn expression changed to concern. "If she doesn't turn up in the next week or so, let's report her as missing. And…let's watch our own backs too."

The whole room went quiet.

Had I made a mistake by coming here?

Gabe got up from his creaky, wooden chair and walked over to a dusty, old shelf that was covered up by a tattered, grey cloth twice its size. He pulled the cloth away and revealed a row of neatly stacked books. Engraved titles such as *'Egypt,'* *'Atlantis'* and *'India'* glowed as bright as candle flames. Gabe ran his fingers across the stack, and pulled out an A3 notebook and some markers.

"Divine, will you be the scribe today?" He asked.

Divine got up from her chair and sat in the middle of the circle, ready to jot down ideas as they flowed.

"Isn't dreaming a bit passive at a time like this?" Hemmy's passion came through his words.

Gabe replied. "The real meaning of dreaming is to be aware of everything around us and to be in full control. It's our mind, our very conscious they've attacked. That's what we need to reclaim. To do this, we need to dream when we're awake and we need to dream when we're asleep."

I was terribly confused.

"Dreaming is the first step towards creating a better life. If we can dream it, we can make it happen. Dreaming gives us strength and determination. It gives us our why. Without it, we feel lost and depressed. Minions feed off this energy and drain us like vampires drain blood from their victims. Dreaming stops this cycle and gives us our power back. It banishes minions and weakens the Demiurge that sends them." Vicki explained.

There was a bolt of lightning outside followed by a loud thunder a moment later. Rain continued to pour heavily. It was as if nature itself had affirmed this.

"So…the ban on dreaming is really a…a ban on our soul?" Michael asked.

Gabe nodded and shared a tried and tested *reality check* method to stimulate dreams and strengthen perception. "Look at your hands or feet. Or try to walk through walls. If nothing happens, you're awake. But if your hands and feet change or if you can walk through walls, you're in a dream." Gabe explained this technique trained our brain to be aware both in waking life and in a dream state, which in turn helped to break down barriers of self-limitation.

I wrote in my notebook: *Dreaming means to be fully aware and to be in complete control. Also, to direct our experiences with intention and focus. This strengthens our mind and prevents others from manipulating us, regardless of whether we are awake or asleep.*

There was another, a more powerful bolt of lightning followed by an even louder thunder.

"I'm thinking of doing a vision quest with Caapi to help with this," Karon said.

"If we're truly ready to listen, oh the things this Amazonian brew can tell us!" Vicki added.

"For those who don't know, Vicki and I have participated in a few Caapi ceremonies. We plan to offer one here next month if you're interested," Gabe said.

"Caapi is a mother's unconditional love and

her absolute wrath, all rolled into one." Vicki laughed.

"Thanks, but no thanks!" JOEL was quick to respond.

"Lemme rephrase it." She chuckled. "Caapi is a plant medicine, or for the lack of a better word, a psychedelic that shuts down the ego part of our mind and lets our soul speak without fear. It also opens doors to spirit-worlds so we can interact with forces greater than ourselves. Amazonians discovered how to make this medicinal brew with two specific plants thousands of years ago."

"How did they know which two plants to mix? There would be at least a hundred thousand plants in those forests." My logic dug deeper.

"That's the ultimate mystery! Amazonians said they learnt it directly from the plant spirits themselves." She replied.

Was this possible?

We continued this discussion for the next twenty minutes.

Gabe closed the meeting by saying, "Please stay behind if you have more questions."

It was already 2120 hours. Where had time flown?! I thanked everyone and left. To be honest, I liked how warm and welcoming they were. But I did not know what to make of the conversation that jumped from one weird topic to the next.

That night, my overstimulated mind kept me awake. The dirty finger of that homeless lady touched my forehead as she screamed, "You n me, n we, n all are cursed; demons live inside us." I tossed and turned. Krishna's Tarot cards flew at me and said, "Your eyes are about to open up to what this world really is." I broke out in sweat and sat up in my bed.

It was only 0445 hours. Wind was whistling and leaves were rustling. Raindrops had gone quiet. Streets were silent. City lights were glowing at a distance and keeping the streetlights of our neighbourhood company. There was stillness in air. But a storm was brewing within my own self.

Mitten was snoring gently at the edge of our bed. I looked at my hands. They remained the same. I got up with soft footsteps and walked over to the study area where my laptop had been charging overnight.

It was time to act. I wrote this email below:

Hi Steven

I will like to thank DR HEATH and yourself for coming to Servitium and giving us an overview of the Dream Catcher study. I look forward to our partnership. Perhaps we can meet for an hour sometime during the week to get the ball rolling?

Regards

Cassandra

By the time I finished, Mitten had woken up and was meowing by my feet demanding breakfast. I filled her bowl with dry biscuits and a couple of treat bites. I myself had a banana and washed it down with some strong coffee.

I left home early that morning and entered the lab at 0715 hours. The whole place was empty as we did not start work until 0800 hours.

As soon as I sat down, EMMA's voice echoed! "…and if they do not do as we say, we will get rid of them."

My ears stiffened. My yawn stopped midway. What was she doing here so early? And who was she talking to?

A man replied. "Only you can be so fierce!"

I froze.

"I cannot have another ANGELO situation." She scoffed.

My mouth went dry. So it really was her I had seen that night just before RYAN was murdered! Actually, I had seen him too. But he could not have stabbed RYAN because he was with me…!

"That Cassandra is a loose cannon as well. Always poking her nose where it does not belong." She continued.

The feeling was mutual, you soulless, empty shell!

"You've got plans for her too, have you?" He teased.

She hissed.

My heart stopped altogether.

Somehow, I forced movement back into my body and packed up my desk with shaking hands. Tingles travelled up and down my spine, and threatened to make me collapse. My pulse picked up pace as my legs limped out of the lab.

I was almost at the lifts when my anxious eyes caught the glimpse of EMMA and Caleb kissing through the half-opened door of her office.

Chapter 9 – The Hermit

My legs wanted to run all the way home. But my autopilot mode carried me into a franchise café across the street. My numb body pulled out a chair in a far corner away from everyone. My shaking hands ordered the first drink that popped up on the self-service screen. And my anxious eyes stared into a distance.

'Only you can be so fierce.' Caleb's words played on my mind. 'I cannot have another ANGELO situation.' EMMA's joined in.

"You're not going to drink that?" A familiar voice jolted me. It was Caleb; his eyes met mine.

What was he doing here? Had he seen me in the lab earlier? Did he know I knew?

"A triple thick-shake filled with cream?" He picked up my glass and narrowed his eyes.

I did not even realise what I had ordered or when it had arrived. Also, eew! Who has that first thing in the morning, or ever?!

Act casual. Smile back. Act casual. Smile back. Act casual. Smile back. My brain kept repeating. I strained a smile at Caleb, who pulled out a chair and sat comfortably in front of me.

"I was craving one." I nervously took a big gulp.

"Well, nothing too adventurous for me. I'll have my boring latte please." He placed his order on the screen.

I forced the artificial, sugary syrup down my throat and pretended to enjoy it.

"Slept well last night?" There was a hint of interrogation in his casual question.

My already clenched gut coiled. The shake was making its way up. With my hand on my mouth, I flew past him and ran to the door. As soon as I was outside and away from the main entrance, I let out a howl and threw up.

"You okay?" He followed me outside and handed me a water bottle.

I rinsed my mouth out a couple of times and said, "All good, just an upset stomach."

"I wonder why! Well, the rest of your drink is still waiting." He seemed amused.

I took a deep breath and wiped my watery eyes.

"Lemme take you home."

"Thanks, but I feel better now."

We went back to the café. Caleb ordered some orange juice to help settle my stomach.

Mixed emotions had me withdrawn. Was he genuinely caring or was he keeping an eye on me?

He took my reserved body language as discomfort from having just thrown up, therefore, sipped his coffee in silence.

From the outside, he seemed like a perfect guy. When did we drift apart and take different directions? Also, had I really been so self-absorbed I had not even noticed?

"Call me if you need anything," he said as we went our separate ways, perhaps for good.

Work that day was restless at best. I did everything I could to avoid EMMA. 'That Cassandra is a loose cannon.' 'You've got plans for her too, have you?' The words kept haunting me.

I sent this message to the only person I could think of: *Hi Richard, hope Laura wasn't too upset yesterday. Tell her I said hi.*

A few minutes later, he replied: *Oh kiddo, she's still mad. It'll pass.*

Best not to disturb him. I went back to work hoping to finish at least one thing.

Just when I was able to focus, Steven appeared at my desk. "Coffee?" He asked.

"I didn't know you were here today...!"

He ran his fingers through his sandy hair and smiled. "I had a meeting with PROF AMON and EMMA BECKER. Thought to say a quick hello to you too."

"How did it go?"

"Meh! The usual. Do this; do more; do faster."

The story of our lives, whether we are villains or heroes or plebs.

We walked to an uptown café a block away. Steven bought us coffees despite my insistence to pay for mine.

"Sorry, I haven't replied to your email yet. We're in the middle of finalising our trials. I haven't even had a decent sleep lately."

"All good! How's it coming along?"

"Interesting, to say the least. How's your chip coming along?"

"So far so good, except for one tricky participant. The secondary investigator in my study, Dr Sara Berry, is monitoring her closely to make sure we remain on track. I'm looking after all others."

Our coffees arrived. A *smile and click* later, I

asked. "Were you always interested in dreams?"

"Nah! My real interest is in cryonics. Do you know much about it?"

"Only bits n pieces."

"Well…at this point, there isn't much happening anyway. As everyone knows, our body gets damaged quickly after death. Since different parts of the body have different freezing temperatures, it's impossible to freeze the entire body at an optimal temperature within the critical timeframe."

I could hear disappointment in Steven's voice.

"In other words, death does damage to our body. Then we cause further damage by trying to freeze it…?" I repeated in my own words.

"Exactly! That's why we haven't been able to revive even one person successfully. Preserving brain or body in a cryonic solution will never work. So, we did the next best thing. We modified microchips to record thoughts and memories of our subjects."

"You turned the chip into a memory card and saved the data that is life? I'm speechless!" I really was. But more at the prospect of continuing on like a virtual vampire.

"Yes. When some of these subjects died, we uploaded their microchips onto a computer hoping to make their consciousness live."

"How did you end up here then?"

"Well…coz we failed. Yes, we managed to save a person's life onto a microchip. But the files weren't aware. We couldn't download the actual consciousness. Maybe coz a microchip isn't the right tool for it…? We decided to wait until the nanochip was launched. Then our funding ran out. We were forced to park this project. Around that time, DEE approached me to co-lead the Dream Catcher study with her. I said yes coz it's a great opportunity to learn about human consciousness, which is the missing link in cryonics as well." Steven's eyes looked straight into mine.

Blood rushed to my cheeks and made them warm. I broke our eye contact and reached for another sip of my coffee.

"Have you found this missing link yet?"

"Not entirely. All I know is…I mean…I'm convinced we're subconsciously interacting with something out there. And that something's signalling back to us through dreams. Case in point the famous mathematician Ramanujan who saw most of his equations in his dreams! Or Einstein who came up with e equals m c square in a daydream!"

"There's certainly more to dreams than meets the eye. Why else would our body burn energy to produce them when it's already made other parts like wisdom teeth, appendix and tonsils redundant?" I added my two cents and thought to also mention the Dreaming group but decided to get to know Steven better first.

"That's why we can't let go of dreams altogether. I don't understand the context of the ban but this is DEE and my own way to challenge it. If we can use dreams to our advantage, who knows, maybe we can all be Ramanujans and Einsteins!"

"If this is the case, is it a good idea to disconnect ourselves from natural dreams and replace them with something artificial and controlled?"

"Inspiration doesn't come naturally to everyone. Us humans need to reboot every night anyway. Why not do so by downloading a safe program of our choice that'll enhance our abilities?"

As we were on the last sips of our coffees, Steven's phone rang. "Excuse me; it's DEE."

He went to a quiet corner to take the call.

Steven's project involved the hacking of human mind. On the one hand, not only did I understood it but also supported it. But on the other hand, I had reservations just like I did with my own nanochip.

He returned a few minutes later and said, "I've gotta go. But let's discuss more over next coffee."

"As long as I'm buying." I took the final sip and put the mug down.

Over the next two days, I worked from home. Locking yourself in a room and forgetting the world is the best way to be productive. I managed to do a full day's worth in just a few hours. This meant more time for chasing Mitten around the house and cuddling afterwards.

Caleb was still at the back of my mind. But I managed to push him further and further away until Tuesday evening when he sent this text: *Everything okay?*

I could not ignore him any longer. It would only strengthen his suspicion. Therefore, after a few minutes, I replied: *Sorry, just getting through a deadline. Let's talk once I'm done.*

He wrote back immediately: *I can bring dinner tonight. It'll save you cooking.*

I lied: *Thanks but I have leftovers.*

He wrote: *Let's do brunch at Mango Moksha this Saturday then.*

I delayed the inevitable and wrote back: *Let's. Goodnight.*

I paced up and down the living room while biting my nails. Who could I speak to about something as sensitive as this? I picked up my phone and typed: *Hope Laura and you are well. I'm working from home tomorrow in case you were around for coffee?* I pressed *send* and waited. Nothing happened. I obsessively checked my screen every two seconds for the next few minutes. No response came back. Of course, I could not expect Richard to be glued to his phone just because I was to mine!

I put my phone away and refilled Mitten's bowl with some dry biscuits. I had to put her on a diet because she had gained weight. Her painful eyes looked at me as if I had just served poison. I wanted to kiss her and open the biggest ever can of tuna. But I remained strong. It was for her own good. I turned my back while she let out whimpering meows, and prepared my dinner of coconut yogurt with granola, almonds and protein powder. How could I justify having a hot meal when my only child forced down cold biscuits?

After finishing my meal, I pulled Adam's diary out from my drawer. I sipped rosehip tea and turned the page to where I had left off last. It read: *Shadows, what are you really? Are you alive or dead or in-between? You hide in corners and watch us. You play with our emotions, heart and even soul.*

An eeriness crept over me. I put the diary down and turned all lights on. When I picked it back up, I skimmed through the next few pages where he had scribed details of his everyday life. Soon, I was on the last page, which read: *I want to make this known in case something happens to me. If I die, it will not be an accident or a suicide. It will be a murder.*

Whaaaaat?!?

My eyes became wide. Was this another one of ADAM's crazy rants or was there truth to it? Regardless, I could not keep this to myself! I had to tell this to the authorities…. or maybe first to Gabe and Karon? Perhaps at our next meeting…? As I contemplated my options, I fell into a troubled sleep.

I woke up the next morning with a throbbing headache. Loud bumps and bangs were coming from the corridor outside and made my ache worse. Someone was either moving in or out of the building. It was pain of a hangover without fun of alcohol.

To drown those unsavoury sounds, I commanded Avantika.R to put on a music track. Soon, the voices accompanying that commotion became louder. I turned the music down and listened closely. Richard and Laura were arguing.

I opened the main door and poked my head outside. Laura was in the corridor with a bunch of boxes.

"You're over-reacting!" She said to Richard while he was on the phone.

He ignored her.

"Fine! You can go. I'm not leaving." She became frustrated at his lack of response.

"We're both leaving, and NOW! We've got a long way to go. Pack as much as you can. Removalists will be here soon," he said as soon as he got off the phone.

"This is complete madness, even for you!" She protested.

I took hesitant steps towards them.

Laura broke into tears as soon as she saw me.

"Richard wants us to move out this very morning! He's already sold our expensive furniture, and for a poor price too. Removalists are coming to pick everything up."

"But…we just had brunch a couple of days ago! You didn't mention a word about this." Suddenly, my hands became cold.

"It's been a long time coming, kiddo. Laura knows exactly why." He shot her an angry look.

"Why…?" I was upset.

"The Grid…." Richard began speaking.

Laura cut him short with her raised voice. "Oh, stop it!"

"You stop it!"

"Okay, I'm sorry! Can we just stay?"

He looked at me and took a deep breath before saying, "We need to go. It's for the best."

Tears rolled down my flushed cheeks.

"Please don't…" My voice trembled. It got drowned in the ringing of pots and pans getting slammed in boxes.

I went back to my apartment and stood outside the door where Mitten was waiting with her low tail. I picked her up and watched Richard pack like a machine while Laura tried to talk him out of it. I did not help. I wanted to make it difficult for them to leave, even if by ever so slightly.

Shortly after, removalists arrived. The whole apartment became empty within minutes. Richard locked the door for the last time. Both him and Laura came up to me. All our eyes were red. They kissed my forehead and gave Mitten a pat.

Richard placed his hands on my shoulders, looked at me and quivered. "Take care of yourself."

"You don't have to go. Whatever it is, I can help."

He turned around without saying a word.

Laura held onto me tightly. A minute later, the lift arrived at our floor and made a *ding*. She looked at me one last time and turned around too.

They left the building, the town and my life. It was not even 0900 hours yet, and I was both angry and sad.

I closed the door behind. My phone was buzzing. But I was in no state to answer it.

What was happening to me? What was happening around me?

As Richard and Laura drove off, Krishna's words rang in my ears. '...it won't be easy and you'll feel alone. Also, someone will leave your life.'

Chapter 10 – The Wheel of Fortune

Yesterday, I had woken up to Richard and Laura's sudden departure. Would they have even said goodbye had I not stumbled upon their loud noises on my own? This thought played on my mind in a loop while Krishna's words echoed in the background. '…it won't be easy and you'll feel alone. Also, someone will leave your life.'

Today, Caleb forced himself into my thoughts. How long had he known EMMA for? Also, how could I trust him now? I cancelled our brunch through a message: *Sorry but feeling unwell and can't catch up tomorrow. Rain check?*

He did not even bother to reply.

On Saturday, EMMA sent this message: *Meeting. Monday 9 am. Don't be late.*

Could there be a plausible explanation behind what I had overheard, and the meeting was to clear the misunderstanding? My thoughts swung from fearful to wishful and kept me up for most of the night. I stared at my hands over and over. Unfortunately, they did not change once.

On Sunday, I woke up miles away from myself. As I was tossing and turning, Laura's voice echoed and gave me a tinge of pain. 'When we chant AUM, its vibration spreads though our entire body and calms our mind."

I peeled myself away from my bed, washed my face and brushed my teeth. Mitten stopped crunching on dry biscuits and meowed for wet food. After opening a low-fat jelly tube for her, I dragged a yoga mat out and forced it on the floor.

Just as I sat in a lotus position, a scraping from the outside confronted my ears and disrupted my non-existent focus some more.

I peeked into the hallway to see what was going on. The door of Richard and Laura's apartment was open. Had Richard changed his mind and were they back already?

"Like, can you put it there pretty please," a woman said.

"Yes ma'am." An electronic voice replied.

"Thank you." She chirped.

A five foot tall humanoid robot walked past me with a trolley. A man was giving it instructions.

"Hi, I'm PEARL." The woman saw me and extended her neatly manicured hand. She was in her early twenties, and had olive skin, high cheekbones, red lips and dark hair extensions.

This was a quick turn-around of tenants. When exactly did Richard give the notice to vacate?

"Hi PEARL, welcome to the building. I'm Cassandra. I live just down the hall." I made myself smile and shook her hand. My chipped nails stood out against her perfect pink. My worn-out pyjamas were a stark contrast to her short, pink designer dress.

"Good morning, Ms Cassandra." The robot greeted me.

I nodded.

"And I'm JADE. Nice to meet you." Another

woman came from inside. I pinched myself because she looked exactly like PEARL! Except for her cream top and denim shorts.

"Ummmm hi JADE, I'm Cassandra, the…the n-neighbour down the hall…" This deja-vu made me stutter. Also, it reinforced who I really was, which was just another neighbour.

They laughed. "We're identical twins. The only way to tell us apart is through this mole near PEARL's right brow."

The removalist man brushed his elbow against one of the twins while lingering his glance on her face and biting his lower lip. That twin giggled.

Richard and Laura had truly moved out. The spinning wheel had stopped at PEARL and JADE. What was this new chapter going to bring?

I went back to my apartment, had a shower and got dressed in a pale blue top and a black knee-length skirt. While having coffee, I resumed my search on the Demiurge. Pages upon pages of irrelevant results came up including d-grade rock bands who had used variations of this name. An hour later, I finally stumbled upon the one page I was after. It had a disclaimer, which stated: *approximate translation only of an ancient text*. It read:

Sophia, a goddess-type being, gave birth to a monstrous child, the Demiurge. She was so ashamed she covered him in a blanket made of clouds and left him. The Demiurge grew up alone and had no awareness of anyone else, not even the true God.

The Demiurge is the architect of the Earth and rules over it.

Wow! I leaned back into the couch. According to this mythology, Demiurge was an unwanted child who carried wounds of abandonment. No wonder he created the only thing he knew and passed these wounds onto the rest of us! Now every child on Earth including you and me, to a greater or a lesser extent, feels the betrayal Demiurge himself once felt.

Compassion replaced fear in my heart and took my focus away from my pain. Did I believe this myth? Not entirely. But it certainly explained a lot about the emotional construct of our world.

I finished the last sips of my coffee and called a cab. Within minutes, I was underneath the neon sign again: *World Renowned* Gypsy *Psychic.* The shop's door read: *Opening hours Tuesday to Sunday– 12 midday to 9 pm.*

I had an hour to spare and nothing to do. Therefore, I went to explore the local area.

The Rheedam of that day was sunny and buzzing. It was a stark contrast to the Rheedam of that other night, which was dark and abandoned. Today, castaway seers dressed in rainbow shades and with eccentric hair were wandering around in a boulevard. It was the same boulevard I had turned into while trying to find shelter from rain a few months ago. Stalls from local business owners were in every corner. One could buy anything homemade, such as coffee, tea and juices; cakes, breads, cheeses, honey and jams; candles, soaps, lotions and oils; clothes and jewelry; and paintings and sculptures. Secondhand books, CDs and records were abundant. Probiotics and iodine were at every third stall. Local musicians took turns to sing their creativity while a cartoonist drew caricatures in a far corner.

This market was violating at least twenty safety protocols, including the limit of how many people could attend one gathering; noise restrictions in a public area; and regulations around selling health supplements and homemade goods.

No organics ever visited this place. The seers here had outright refused the microchip, unlike me who was forced to do so due to an anaphylactic reaction. How funny though, that here we were, all together as if we were the same!

While my mind noted these breaches and differences, my eyes caught a small painting of a spiral disc filled with shooting stars and dancing lights. "Andromeda!" I whispered. I could not help but walk towards it, and before I knew, I had parted with thirty En-GYs. The street artist carefully wrapped it in a brown paper and handed it to me. I tucked it under my arm and made my way to the food area where people were lined up for dumplings, samosas, tacos, salads and falafels. My stomach growled and reminded me I had barely eaten the whole week. I joined in and bought one crunchy, spicy samosa filled with potatoes and peas; and a small baked falafel ball on a bed of pickled carrots and cabbages. I washed these down with fresh orange juice and relaxed to a catchy tune that was being played by a local musician.

Yes, this completely different world had sucked me in. I forgot my own audit from not too long ago and bought more goodies. Specifically, a jar of raspberry and chia seeds jam, a loaf of sourdough bread, two frangipani soaps and some candles. No-one said, "Smile and click." Instead, these castaways showed genuine interest in how my week had been. Also, one gypsy-looking woman gave me a free healing to balance something in my body. I was too polite to refuse. When I tried to pay afterwards, she said, "Consider it a gift from the Universe." It was nice, even if a little weird.

Soon it was midday. The sign flashed blue and red. I rinsed my hands under a nearby water tap and made my way to the shop. Krishna was still drawing curtains and setting up his table when I knocked on the door. He was once again in skinny jeans and a loose-fitting shirt.

"Welcome back." He smiled.

He remembered me?

"Thanks. I was in the neighbourhood so thought to drop by." I did not want him to know I had come specifically for him.

He lit a lavender stick and handed me a deck of Tarot cards. "Please take a seat and shuffle."

Once I finished, he laid the cards in a fan and asked me to pick any six.

I did.

He closed his eyes, took a deep breath and said, "The first card represents the immediate past. For you, it's the Eight of Cups. Leaving all behind and moving on. Someone has left your life. Or you're leaving your old self behind. Or both. Painful but necessary."

I was surprised he had picked up on Richard and Laura's departure.

"The next two cards represent the present. The High Priestess and the Page of Cups. Hmmm… your intuition is getting strong. Your subconscious is sending you messages. Maybe you will have a-" He coughed and stopped mid-sentence.

Was he really about to say what I think he was?

He cleared his throat and continued. "There's love around you. He's very intelligent and has a mind of science."

The only person who matched this description

was Caleb. But after last week, we could never be.

Krishna's expression became solemn as he read the remaining three cards. "These represent future over the next four months. The Tower, the Seven of Swords and the Empress. You'll be betrayed by a trusted friend. Also, life will demand a sacrifice. But don't worry. In the end, everything will be okay."

I picked up the Empress card, which was a picture of a beautiful woman sitting on a royal, red throne in a blossoming garden.

Krishna closed the reading. I paid him fifty En-GYs.

I got up to leave.

"Will you like some tea?" He asked.

There was something oddly comforting about this bearer of bad news. Therefore, even though my belly was full from lunch, I said, "Sure, thanks."

He put a *busy* sign on his door and took out a tin can and two cups from a small wooden cupboard in the kitchenette area. He rinsed the cups, filled them with some dried leaves and boiled water in an old kettle. Once ready, he poured the water in the two cups. Earthy aroma of the tea joined smoke of the lavender.

"What is it?" I asked.

"Mugwort."

"I've never had it before."

"It stimulates our brain." He winked and placed the two brewing cups between us. Silence accompanied the next few moments, where neither him nor I said a word.

"I searched for your business online but couldn't find anything." I broke the ice.

"I like to keep a low profile." He got up and

brought a jar of honey from the wooden cupboard.

"This must've cost you a fortune!" We did not have bees anymore, which made honey rare and priceless.

"That's why I bring it out only for special guests."

I smiled awkwardly and added a tiny dollop to my cup. The bitterness of mugwort turned into sweetness.

"Got much planned for the week?" He asked.

"Not really. Just work, a dinner and time with my cat Mitten. How about yourself?"

"Same, but no cat."

My cup was still half-full. I said, "I'm sorry."

He gave me a confused look. Another fragment of conversation died just as quickly. The next few moments were filled with our sips.

"How did you get into this line of work? Most people would think of it as nothing more than a gimmick." I broke the silence again.

"Yet I have loyal customers who keep coming back." He laughed.

At me?

He picked up the Tarot and laid some cards out. "These inanimate pictures, they speak to me. And through them, I'm able to tell others what they need to know. For example, you need to know that mugwart is good for...dreaming."

I gasped! He sure had figured out a lot. Was he a real psychic or just another mentalist?

"Your secret's safe with me. Lightening's striking your tower. But at least you're not alone."

Lightening was striking my tower! The life I had built so carefully was crumbling away. Random events and unwanted paranormal experiences were taking over, which was making me doubt my sanity.

"Were you alone?" I read between the lines and asked.

Suddenly, a gush of wind entered his carefully enclosed shop. It blew all the candles off and ripped a few cards from the fanned Tarot deck. We turned to the door in case a passerby had opened it. But there was no one.

We were perplexed and looked at each other.

Krishna re-lit the candles. I picked up the three cards on the floor. The first was a young person walking with a dog; both were about to fall off a cliff. The second had a deep red heart with three swords pierced in it. The final was a dark horned entity that had a couple in chains.

I handed these cards to him. He looked at each of them for a long minute and sighed. "My Tarot seems to trust you. Maybe I can use a friend after-all..."

I gave him a reassuring smile. We sat down and sipped more tea.

We discussed general sentiment of growing up under the Grid's watchful eyes and losing our individualities in the process. A few minutes later, he opened up on a deeper level.

"I was born into a community...well no...a cult really...where everyone was a narcissist. They thought they were gods-"

"But aren't we the gods, the creators of our lives, for better or worse?" I interjected.

"That's different. Yah, we're responsible for our thoughts and actions, and the consequences they bring. And yah...with our will, we can accomplish what we want. We have the ability to create. But that doesn't make us the Creator."

I nodded while struggling to see how this technicality affected Krishna's life.

He continued. "My parents, just like everyone else in that cult, were too busy doing low-level rituals to attract holidays and designer things. They lived in a bubble of 'positive thoughts' where everything was about them. Me, me, me. Selfishness at its most! They constantly shifted the goalpost of what was right or wrong to suit their purpose by saying, 'it's all an experience' and 'do not judge.' They didn't even protect me. They looked away when...when...when their own friends hurt me..." His voice quivered towards the end. His eyes became teary.

I took his hands into mine. My own eyes had mist too.

Krishna took a big gulp. "I wasn't the only one either. Many children were. I left as soon as I turned sixteen and never looked back."

I held his hand tighter. "You're very strong. Most wouldn't have made it out."

"Most didn't..."

"Did the Family Branch not help?"

He did not say a word.

I wanted to ask more but the heaviness in the room told me not to.

Krishna excused himself to go to the restroom, which was at the back of his shop. I wiped my eyes and took a deep breath.

I felt for him. In fact, I felt for every adult who had survived and every child who was still helpless. How could people not see it is risky to live in their own little bubbles?! It disconnects us from the suffering of others, which leaves the vulnerable to fend for themselves. If this is not Social Darwinism, then what is?

I got up, boiled more water and topped up our cups. Krishna came back a few minutes later. He took a sip of his tea and changed the topic. "Your cards suggest you're in a bit of a pickle. What's going on?"

My fear of shadows had temporarily disappeared after reading the Demiurge myth. Therefore, I downplayed seeing ghoulish entities every now and then.

Krishna jumped up. "Don't take it lightly! I know someone who can help. He used to be a doctor but runs a group now." He reached for his phone to get details.

"Gabe?" My face let out an expression.

"You know him?" He was surprised.

I raised my left eyebrow and shifted from one leg to another.

Turned out, we both knew Gabe. Him and Krishna had met a few years ago when Gabe was still in depression, having lost his career as a radiologist. Krishna had only just moved here after completing a degree in Arts and was opening up this very shop. They were acquaintances who almost became business partners. But Gabe wanted to set up a formal group and organise events to raise awareness. Krishna, on the other hand, "needed time-out to heal." Hence, they wished each other the best and parted ways, maintaining only intermittent contact.

"I should check out Gabe's group. It's long overdue," he said.

"We're meeting tonight. Maybe I'll see you there?"

"Maybe…"

I sipped the last drop of my tea, thanked him and left.

How utterly fragmented yet coincidentally connected our lives can be. Of all the places where I was an outsider, I belonged here the most. I was getting addicted to all things strange.

Chapter 11 – The Justice

That evening was my second meeting with the Dreaming group. At 1830 hours, I was back in Gabe's attic amid dancing candle flames and rare books. He was wearing a peach collared shirt with grey pants and greeted me with a childish grin.

"Something smells delicious." I took a breath of the pine-nut and coriander air.

"Thank you!" He smiled.

As per the protocol, I turned my phone off and left it downstairs in the designated spot. After this, Gabe led me to the attic upstairs.

Hemmy, who wore khaki shorts and a navy polo shirt, sat a few meters away on a stack of weights. JOEL towered over him in denim jeans and a black collared shirt. They were deep in a conversation. I did not interrupt. Instead, I pulled out a protein bar from my handbag to munch on, and thought about ADAM's diary and RYAN's note.

"Wow Gabe, you've outdone yourself tonight." Karon's voice broke my thoughts. She wore a green sweater, black pants and a rainbow scarf. Her blond and purple hair was pinned back tightly in a small bun, which revealed her leaf-shaped gold earrings.

Divine entered the attic wearing an oversize burgundy shirt and black jeans. She looked at my pale pink dress with grey butterflies and said, "I have it in green!" We laughed and decided to go out one night in our matching dresses.

Soon, Michael joined us in a deep blue jumper and dark jeans. Before we knew, the whole room was buzzing.

A skinny frame with blond hair entered and placed a big iron cast pot on the bench. Gabe clapped to get our attention. "Hi everyone, this is my friend Krishna. He's our guest tonight."

Krishna wore his signature skinny jeans and a loose-fitting, pale shirt. His hair was pulled high in a ponytail, which looked more chic than mine.

"We've prepared a vegetable and bean soup. The vegetables are from Krishna's own garden. Please help yourselves." Gabe cheered.

The room echoed from "thank you" to "what a rebel."

We lined up for a medley of carrots, celery and cannellini beans. My first spoonful introduced me to a harmony of ginger and tomatoes. What a perfect soup for dreamers on a cold evening.

Vicki was the last one to arrive. As soon as she entered the room, her lime green coat with blue stars caught everyone's attention. She walked up to Gabe and whispered, "Ready?"

He nodded. She rang a bell. We took seats in a circle laid out for us. Krishna sat next to me. We did not need a Tarot deck or EN-GYs to connect anymore. A genuine friendship had formed between us.

"How does one grow their own vegetables?" My question was really a compliment.

"Start with tomatoes; they're the easiest." Was his tip.

Growing one's own food became illegal in late 2020s due to a risk of contamination, which meant thirty years later, we all had two black thumbs.

Gabe cleared his throat and said, "We've organised a Caapi ceremony for this Friday the thirteenth. If you're interested, please let us know."

"I'm in!" Karon screamed and bounced.

"Count me in as well." Michael put his hand up.

Krishna and I exchanged a glance. Caapi was not my cup of tea. Was it his?

"You have till Wednesday to confirm. I'll stay behind again tonight in case you have questions." Vicki concluded and got up for a serve of the soup.

"Now onto our main business." Gabe passed around a small bamboo basket.

One by one, we put neatly folded pieces of paper inside. The "main business" comprised of two key questions he had asked us to consider via an encrypted group chat a few days ago. First, how do you feel about dreams? And second, have you had any? Instead of saying anything out loud, because a few of us were relatively new and nervousness still reigned, Gabe had told us to write our answers down on paper so we could discuss them under a veil of relative anonymity.

My responses read: *I'm still figuring out how I feel about dreams; and I have not had one yet. But I do see shadows. What exactly are these?*

After everyone dropped their paper in, Gabe began his talk. "When we fall into a deep sleep, our brain activity increases and our eyes move quickly. This is known as rapid eye movement sleep, or REM sleep. Theoretically, this is the best time to have dreams. The million-dollar question is: how can we make the most of it?"

"We can't!" Michael exclaimed.

Gabe raised his eyebrows and laughed. "That's what we're led to believe. But we shouldn't underestimate ourselves. Dreamers back in the day practiced a five-step technique called wake back to bed, or WBTB. It helped to stimulate not just any dreams but dreams in which one was fully conscious. Lucid dreams!"

"Lucid dreams are a myth." Divine shrugged her shoulders.

"Why don't you practice this technique for a few weeks, then tell me!" Gabe smiled. He gave us the following instructions to induce a lucid dream:

- Step 1 - Set a clear intention. Say out loud before going to bed, "I will myself to dream tonight."
- Step 2 - Set an alarm for five hours after your bedtime. For example, if you are going to bed at ten, set an alarm for three the next morning.
- Step 3 - Go to sleep.
- Step 4 - When the alarm goes off at three, fight the temptation of turning it off and continuing to sleep. Instead, wake up and stay awake for thirty minutes. Read or write or listen to soft music and do nothing strenuous.
- Step 5 - Go back to sleep after the thirty minutes.
- And observe your hands or feet regularly. If they change, you are in a dream. If they

do not, you are not. This is known as a *reality check.*

"How does WBTB even work?" I asked.

"For the thirty minutes we're awake, as long as we don't do anything strenuous, our brain activity remains as if we're still in a deep sleep. This gives us the best of both worlds and increases our probability of going straight into a REM sleep when we close our eyes." Gabe replied.

"You mean…by keeping our mind alert at a time when we would otherwise be sleeping, we train ourselves to become more aware…?" I repeated in my own words.

Gabe nodded. 'This helps us to be conscious in dreams and also have heightened senses when awake."

"Have you tried this yourself?" JOEL asked.

"Why else would I be teaching it? It took its time, but I finally had a breakthrough. Our brain's like plastic. With right techniques and enough discipline, we can mould it to learn new skills." Gabe replied.

We continued to discuss dreaming for the next hour. Everyone took down notes. Mine read:

The WBTB technique sharpens our senses both when we are asleep and when we are awake. This is a major step towards reclaiming our energy and taking back control of our consciousness so it cannot be manipulated by fear or propaganda.

After Gabe finished, we had a five-minute break to use restrooms and refill our bowls. When I returned, he was showing Krishna pages out of a blue notebook.

"There's something cathartic about writing things down. They also stick in our mind better," he said when he saw me looking over. I took it as a cue and joined in.

The notebook pages had scribbles in red, green and blue ink. Dotted and solid lines connected various points together. "Is this a mind-map of something?" I asked.

"Of our next topic." He replied.

Krishna was flabbergasted. "You're not going to talk about demonic possessions, are you?"

"No. But I'm counting on you to!" He winked.

I looked at them with confused eyes.

"I can't!" Krishna cried.

"Your experiences are valuable. I'll support you." Gabe replied, then said loudly, "Time to reconvene."

Within a minute, we were back in our seats.

"Being a radiologist was good for me." Gabe chortled with a hint of sadness. "It taught me not to take anything at face value and to assess everything with a scientific rigour. After much research, I've arrived at a few conclusions. These also relates to a question two of you have asked. What are shadows?"

He had picked my question! My heart jumped. But who was the second person? I looked around but no-one gave anything away. I hoped I had not either.

"Earth is a concrete, three-dimensional reality. To experience life here, our soul, which is made of light, needs to connect strongly with our body, which is made of matter. What happens if our soul and body vibrate at different frequencies and don't connect properly with each other?" He asked.

"We feel spaced out," Vicki said.

"And…?" He pressed.

"We get tired easily, become accident prone and need more sleep," Divine said.

"If we go one step deeper, what else?"

There was silence.

"Okay, lemme put it another way. Say you have a house. But you don't spend enough time there. And when you are there, you don't use the kitchen or bathroom or living room. What will happen to that house?"

"It'll collect dust. Appliances can stop working," I said.

"And…?"

"Cockroaches, spiders and mould appear." JOEL added.

"Exactly! Now let's apply this principle to ourselves. If our soul doesn't 'own' it's home, which is our body, what can happen?" He looked directly at Krishna.

We all joined in and did the same.

Krishna hesitated for a moment before speaking in a low and deep voice. "We become an empty vessel. A breeding ground for possessions."

"As in d-demonic?" Hemmy asked.

Krishna nodded. "If we won't take control of our body, someone or something else will."

Hemmy flinched and pushed his chair back. Divine let out a shriek. Michael's eyes opened wide. My own heart picked up pace. Silence accompanied the next few minutes. Was this leading up to gaunt shadows?

Krishna cleared his throat and shifted in his chair. "The more trauma we endure, the weaker our energy becomes. If we don't focus on healing ourselves, we become a target of evil. I experienced this myself when my own pain made me escape into occult." He spoke eloquently but his distress was visible.

We could hear a pin drop.

"Time for a short break." Gabe attempted to break the heavy mood. Him and Krishna got up and went to a corner. The rest of us dispersed. Divine, Karon and I collected used spoons, bowls and cups, and loaded them in the dishwasher downstairs. JOEL tapped on Hemmy's shoulder and soon, both were stretching their arms and legs. Vicki and Michael took turns to use the restroom.

A few minutes later, Gabe's clapping brought us back. He said, "Technically, the problem isn't with the occult itself. It's the dark spirits one can conjure through it. Then there's an issue of too much information; us humans just don't know how to handle it. That's why it's best not to delve into the unknown unless we have a strong soul and body connection."

The room was under a spell of silence. My sceptic mind wanted to fight what Gabe and Krishna were saying. But my own recent experiences had alerted me to another, a more sinister world out there. I listened and waited for answers that made sense to me.

Krishna said, "I was young, in pain and couldn't discern. I nearly lost my life. Thankfully, an exorcist helped me. When I was free, I packed my bags, left town and moved here."

"My friends, certain things are definitely real; even though they may be rare." Gabe looked directly at us one by one.

I struggled to believe my ears. If I had not gotten to know Krishna beforehand, I would have doubted his credibility and dismissed his experience as a psychotic episode.

"I learnt a lot from that horrible part of my life. Mainly, that our physical body and soul have different energies coz one has an expiry date; the other is forever. Trauma creates a divide between the two. On top of that, we modify our body for health and cosmetic reasons. Yah, these help us but their side-effects wear us down. Then of course there's radiation, the AI field and microchips, which interfere with our energies. Imagine the combined impact of these! If we don't put conscious effort towards healing our issues, it's only a matter of time before our mind betrays us. This lets something else come in n take over."

Gabe gave Krishna a reassuring look. We all thanked him for sharing his story.

"The microchip, or should I say, technology, is it a possession?" Michael asked.

Gabe replied. "There's a fine line between improving ourselves and losing ourselves. In fact, the problem isn't even the chip; it's us humans. Why? Coz most of us are emotionally fractured. But instead of healing ourselves, we've escaped into a virtual world and made our soul redundant."

Fractured. Yes, we all are fractured because of one reason or another.

"The worst of us have turned into organics. But mind you, even us seers are walking a thin line. Coz we don't listen to our soul or body anymore," Karon said.

"In other words, if we won't take control of our body, some wandering entity or demon out there will. And our soul won't be able to fight back coz it never had a strong enough connection with our body to begin with!" Gabe reinforced.

What a perfect matrix this is! Be born in the

Demiurge's world, endure trauma as a child, never fully recover, escape into addictions and make our soul an easy target for whatever was out there.

"So demonic possessions really are real?" JOEL panicked.

"Sadly, yes." Gabe replied.

"I would rather be possessed by a chip than a demon." JOEL laughed nervously.

"What if one opens the door for another? Did you know until fifty years ago, even though our world was in a terrible state, actual possessions were extremely rare? Dark entities lurked in corners but our physical was so strong they could never ever touch us. Now, with an explosion in virtual reality, our energies, or auric shields as we call them, have become weak. Without even realising, we've relinquished control of our lives and offered ourselves up on a silver platter." Krishna gave us goosebumps.

"AI could've really made our lives easier. But we've turned it into another dark weapon. Have you ever felt touch and tingles as you go to sleep?" Vicki asked.

Yes!

I looked around. Every face was in panic.

"These low-level, parasitic shadows…to their credit, have unlimited patience. They've waited for millenniums for us humans to dig our graves with our own hands. Now all they need is to push us in them," Krishna said.

I *was* being pushed to my grave! I could feel it.

"Just like a television or a radio has multiple channels, our Universe has multiple worlds. We're all separated by frequencies. When we alter our sense of awareness, whether consciously or subconsciously, we alter our frequency and can tap into other worlds. Equally, beings of these worlds can interact with us by changing their own frequency. It's the same as changing channels on a television," Vicki said.

"And if our soul's connection with our body is weak, these beings can manipulate our frequencies to their advantage. They can turn this interaction into interference. In extreme circumstances, they can also possess us. I repeat Krishna's words. If our own soul won't claim our body, something else will! The effects won't always be supernatural like in horror movies; they can manifest as health problems too coz every disease is an ailment of a soul," Gabe said.

"But how does dreaming fit into this? Shouldn't we be learning about exorcism then?" Hemmy asked.

"There are countless malicious entities out there. How many exorcisms can one do? Also, what's wiser? To spend all our energy killing every parasite in the world? Or to spend a tiny fraction of that energy cleaning our own body and home?" Gabe asked.

The whole room went under a spell of silence.

I picked at the dry cuticles on my nails and opened up the conversation again. "This would mean there's no such thing as bad luck; only a lack of connection, which creates health, money and relationships problems, and makes us feel hexed."

"Exactly! That's why we need to strengthen our awareness during waking hours, which is about two-thirds of our life. Also, we need to strengthen our awareness during sleeping hours, which is the remaining one-third of our life. Then no-one, living or dead or virtual, can manipulate us," he said.

Vicki jumped up and said, "Hence the Caapi

ceremony! It can help us to free our mind and connect with our soul. It can help us to understand the nature of reality in a way we can't in our everyday state." She went on to tell us certain spiritual sects even believed during birth, DMT, which is Caapi's main ingredient, is released in large proportions through our pineal gland and allows our soul to enter our body. And upon death, we are flooded with DMT once again to open that portal back up so our soul can leave. Also, that DMT is the most frequently occurring neurotransmitter on Earth. All plants have it, as do all animals, and humans including you and me.

"Caapi ceremony mimics a near-death experience. But please think about it before you put your hand up to do one. It can be positive if we're ready. But it can also be negative if we're not. And don't underestimate our dreaming exercises. Yes, they're softer in comparison. But if practiced regularly, they're just as powerful." Gabe concluded the evening.

Some including me dispersed as soon as the meeting finished while others stayed behind.

Was Caapi the way to unscramble my own brain? I had till Wednesday to decide.

I made my way home to Mitten while repeating: *a cockroach moves into an empty or an unclean house*. I was definitely going to remember this. How about *you*?

Chapter 12 – The Hanged Man

That Sunday night, I leapt into my bed while reflecting on my new-found place in the world. Mitten started snoring as soon as I covered her with a Hello Kitty blanket. I placed a Dickensian novel on the side table and looked at my hands. They did not change. I set my alarms to wake up five hours later.

As soon as my head hit the pillow, a dread came over me. Why did EMMA want to meet first thing tomorrow? Did she know I knew? This thought made the night just as restless as the ones before. I tossed and turned until my alarm went off. It was already 0400 hours and any REM activity was miles away. I remained awake and read about the pitiful life of David Copperfield until it was time to get ready for the day.

That morning, I arrived at work terribly tired. As soon as I entered the building, a notification popped up on my phone: *1 new message from the Grid.*

My stabilisers did not need a refill for another two weeks. What else could it be? I opened the email; it read:

> *Dear Cassandra*
>
> *We have received an anonymous tip about some of your recent activities. Briefly, that you harbour anti-Grid sentiment and are romanticising a mental disorder. Our independent investigation deems these allegations to be accurate. Therefore, we have deducted 10 points from your HumanSite account.*

In accordance with the protocol 'Citizen conduct breach G002,' we have also notified your employer, the Servitium.

As you are an intelligent professional and a valued citizen, we hope we can work together to get you back on track. One of our officers will be in touch soon.

Regards

The Grid

My phone slipped out of my hands and fell to the floor. The loss of ten points was equivalent to the punishment for doing a cyber fraud!

The tornado of EMMA came rushing towards me and howled. "In the conference room, now!"

My legs lost all feelings.

"Now!" She barked again.

I looked at my hands hoping they would morph into something else. Unfortunately, they did not.

My heart tightened. I followed EMMA with a hanging head. As soon as I entered the room, PROF DAVE AMON gave me a concerned look. "We received this on Saturday morning." He pushed a piece of paper towards me.

I took a deep breath and read:

Dear PROF DAVE AMON

We regret to advise one of your employees, Dr Cassandra Rees, is under investigation for harbouring anti-Grid sentiments and sympathising with rebels. We have also received an anonymous tip about her interest in the mental disorder of dreaming.

We are forced to take this matter in our hands and expect full cooperation from your end. One of our officials will be in touch soon to discuss further.

Regards

The Grid

I sank into my chair. The room faded into black.

"We should terminate her contract." EMMA's words came at me from a hollow distance.

"Quiet EMMA! I have known Cassandra for years and can at least vouch for her work ethic, if nothing else. Although Cassandra, I am truly disappointed." PROF AMON handed me a glass of water.

My hands were trembling. I could not accept it.

This was completely unfair! Even though I had developed an interest in dreaming, I had neither committed a crime nor let it affect my work. Also, if dreams were indeed so volatile, why did DEE and Steven have funding to study them?

"This is a set-up," I whispered after a long pause.

"Lies!" EMMA screamed.

"This is a set-up." I repeated, this time more firmly. The room came back slowly.

"We cannot trust her! We have to let her go." She persisted.

"We cannot afford to at this critical point!" PROF AMON stared at her and matched her aggressive tone.

She retreated.

When I finally had enough composure to defend myself, I said, "I've never harmed anyone or even thought about it. I even work evenings and weekends to help realise the Grid's vision of the nanochip. How is this anti-Grid and sympathising with rebels?"

PROF AMON softened his voice. "My hands are tied, Cassandra. The only thing I can do is make sure you still have a job here. At least this will help you to retain some credibility. But we will have to put you on probation and monitor your work closely."

PROF AMON had a heart. Or was he just looking after his bottom line? Regardless, I appreciated his support and said, "Thank you."

"And EMMA, I trust you will maintain your professionalism." He was stern.

EMMA scoffed and stomped out.

"Go home and pull yourself together. I will see you tomorrow." PROF AMON opened the door and left me alone.

The dry air continued to chock my throat. My legs melted. I sank even deeper into the chair as darkness closed in.

When I finally felt my legs again, I packed up my desk and left the building. My feet struggled to carry my weight. Every step was an effort. To make matters worse, streets were blocked because a protest was underway. People were dressed in black, wore Dali masks, carried banners and chanted:

No more surveillance. Dreams aren't a mental disorder.

Cops on brown horses followed them closely in case it escalated to violence.

What fools these protesters were! They did not even realise it was not the Grid but the betrayal of their own loved ones they were up against. The loved ones who were spying on their every move, ready to give them up at the first opportunity!

Anger engulfed me. I could hear EMMA and Caleb laughing at me. They had won this round.

I pulled my phone out to scream at Caleb.

Suddenly, a familiar raspy voice said, "Hello

missy, can you spare a quarter?"

My spine tingled. "What's a quarter?" I turned around and asked.

My brown eyes met the green of Cynthia's, the homeless woman who had chased after me months ago and led me to Rheedam and Krishna! This was where it had all started. Would this moment be different if instead of running away, I had faced her that day? Or not crossed paths with her at all?

The woman laughed. The big, round City clock chimed. It turned just as dark and cloudy as that first afternoon when we were here, exactly here.

I took a few steps back and raised my voice. "Don't come near me or I'll create a scene!"

Cynthia's persona changed. She moved her arms and legs in a controlled motion, as if spelling something, and whispered, "Oh…but the scene has already been set on the stage of life. Now it's time to act, young dreamer."

I took the pepper spray out of my handbag and threatened her. She hobbled away while muttering something. I followed her. But she disappeared into the crowd. I was left standing in the middle with Dali protesters and galloping horses on one side and beeping horns on the other.

The next day, I was back at work despite my stripped dignity. People around were polite and professional, albeit more distant. Or was the latter my imagination?

EMMA called me into her office and hissed. "From now on, as soon as you arrive at work, you need to run me through your planned tasks for the day. And before you leave, you need to provide me with an update of what you have done."

I fumed at the thought of being micromanaged by someone whose comprehension and skillset were only a fraction of mine. But I needed to play the game. I bit my tongue and explained the technicalities and challenges of the nanochip. EMMA argued at every point and made recommendations that were neither relevant nor helpful. After an impasse, we brought PROF AMON into the conversation, who had only just finished a meeting. He of course agreed with me, much to the dismay of EMMA's red face. But she did not give up and continued to sting. "By the way, we cannot have the likes of you presenting at our Infinite Potential symposium. Just prepare the slides; I will deliver them."

I stormed out of the room. Did I still want this job? Not particularly. But PROF AMON had been kind despite getting a picture that painted me as a rebel. I could not bail out on him; not now anyway. Also, why should I be the one to leave? Therefore, I went back to the lab and buried myself in my *why*.

Shortly after, Steven tapped on my desk. "Coffee?"

I had no idea he was here today. I dragged words out of my heavy heart. "Sorry, I'm busy."

"C'mon Cassandra, you need a friend, and now more than ever. Also, there's something I need your help with."

I relented. "See you at the lifts in five."

We walked to a nearby café. Last time, he had paid for our coffees. This time, I did despite his insistence not to. In the *smile and click* photo, I looked dead and he looked sharp. We made small conversation about weather and work. After we finished our drinks and walked out, he said, "Sorry…I know it's selfish of me to even ask. But…but you're the only one I could turn to."

I looked straight at him and said, "Sure." My only thought was: *it had better not be for EMMA*.

"There was a meeting this morning. PROF AMON told us your chip will be launched in six weeks. DEE said I'll get only four weeks after that to use it in our study and report on results. But I need more time. I haven't even finished analysing all the data yet!"

"Wait what….? No one discussed this six-week deadline with me!"

What exactly was PROF AMON thinking? Were him and EMMA playing good cop bad cop and planning to toss me aside as soon as I delivered?

"Can you delay it, even if by two weeks?"

"Why will they listen to me after what's happened?"

"Coz you're still here. Anyone else would've been long gone. I can't ask DEE coz I don't think she cares about the study or my warnings about the glitches."

"Glitches?"

"Yes! You'll think I'm crazy…or maybe not. It's hard to explain. Something weird is going on. If I didn't know better, I'd say…hmm…never mind."

My ears perked up. I immediately thought of the microchip barcode from RYAN. Could I use this opportunity to lock in a trade? I was already a rebel as far as others were concerned.

"I'll help. But I need a favour too," I said.

"Sure. What is it?"

"I'll explain later. Also, you need to tell me what this glitch is."

"Finally, someone who wants to listen! Come

to my lab this Saturday night. No-one else will be there."

I hesitated for a moment but agreed.

The next day, when EMMA hissed at me to have the chip finalised in six weeks, I stood my ground. "I need at least nine weeks to make improvements and run tests. We've already invested a lot in it. We can't mess it up at the last minute."

"Arrr...okay! But make it no later. I want to get you out of my life already!"

The feeling was mutual, you soulless crone!

As much as I enjoyed this small win over her, her reaction confirmed I had no future at Servitium. This came as no surprise. All I knew was, it was no coincidence I was in-charge of the nanochip while life was opening my eyes and changing my perspective.

That night as I was getting ready for bed, Vicki's name flashed on my phone. I did not even know she had my number! I answered the call expecting a casual touch-base regarding the upcoming Caapi ceremony, which I had not thought about at all.

As soon as I said, "Hello,' she began sobbing.

"K-Karon's missin' since yesterday. We're searching for her. Have filed a p-police report. Gabe's asked me...t-to call everyone...and let'em know."

"What?"

"Karon's missin'. Be careful...d-dunno how safe the rest of us are...Gabe'll be in touch soon."

My heart sank. My mind went blank.

Chapter 13 – The Death and the Temperance

It takes a lifetime to prepare for death.
We must be patient and surrender with trust.

Vicki's phone-call lasted all of two minutes. But it turned my large living room into a small box and trapped me inside. It gave me terrors of Karon getting stabbed just like RYAN. It made me fear I was next, as were Gabe, Krishna, Vicki, Divine, Michael, Hemmy and JOEL.

I thought of Caleb and wished he was still here. I thought of Richard and Laura, and wished they were still around the corner.

Loud meows filled the room and snapped me back into the *now*. In that moment, I realised who was still here. I closed my eyes and willed that box away. Mitten jumped onto my lap and purred. My breathing returned to normal.

Shortly after, Gabe sent this message: *Please keep Karon in your prayers. Our Friday plan will still go ahead. Now more than ever we need to stand together as one.*

He was right. I could not live in fear any longer; it would only put me in line to be slaughtered. Karon needed me. I needed me. Therefore, I wrote back immediately: *Karon is in my prayers. Please count me in for*

Friday.

Over the next day, I found out the Monday gone, Karon had left for her art studio as usual. But when it was midday and she had still not turned up, her co-workers raised alarm. Vicki, being her emergency contact, was the first to find out. Soon, Gabe got involved and filed a police report. After that, they launched a social media campaign in her search. Everyone in the Dreaming group including myself donated EN-GYs to help it get maximum exposure. When Steven found out, he contributed as well. An unexpected benefit of the campaign was it put us in the public eye, which drastically reduced the odds of us turning up dead ourselves. However, I did have one more point deducted from my HumanSite account; this time for "getting distracted from the Grid's vision." This made work excruciating for a moment. But when PROF AMON realised my productivity was not affected in the slightest, everything went back to its cold and tense self, albeit still minus that one point.

Before I knew, Friday evening came around. As I got ready for the Caapi ceremony, I thought of Karon, who had introduced me to this world. Where was she tonight?

Caapi requires commitment. At least a few weeks before the ceremony, we need to stop taking all drugs and medications including alcohol and stabilisers. Also, at least three days prior, we are required to consume a strict vegetarian diet and abstain from sex. Finally, we need to be empty stomach on the day of the ceremony. All this was no problem for me.

Divine, Hemmy and JOEL had opted out. Divine offered to babysit Mitten while I took part. After I repeated Mitten's food schedule and massage preferences for the fifth time, she laughed and said, "Trust me, I got this!"

Gabe had asked us to arrive an hour early because Krishna was doing a Tarot reading for Karon. When I buzzed the intercom, he opened the door and led me into his living room for the first time. Usually, we would drop our switched off mobile phones in a bowl by the door, go straight to the stairs and climb up to the attic.

The living room walls were layered with large oil paintings in silver frames. One was of a bright blue ocean with white foamy waves; another was of a deep green forest with yellow sunrays and the last was of a desert filled with brown sand dunes. An L-shaped five-seater couch faced glass panes and overlooked the city. Himalayan salt lamps were lit in every corner, giving the room a pink hue.

Gabe's plain tee-shirt and stone-washed jeans gave the impression this was just another casual Friday evening. Krishna's signature skinny jeans, Vicki's brown maxi dress, Michael's grey sweatpants and in fact my own khaki dress with white borders could have fooled anyone. However, the solemn looks on our faces told the truth.

We gathered at the dark ebony six-seating dining table next to the kitchen. Krishna fanned his cards and pulled a few out. "The Queen of Cups, The Tower and the Knight of Swords reversed." He bit his fingernails before continuing. "Karon is represented by the Queen. Kind, creative, intuitive. A man is involved, younger than her. Fast and impulsive; quick to anger. Between them is the Tower. Pain; upheaval; destruction."

"What does this mean?" Gabe asked while

searching for clues in those pictures.

Krishna pulled out another card; this time of a horned entity that had a couple entangled in chains. I remembered it from my own readings. "Let's ramp up our efforts and keep praying." He replied.

Michael and I looked at each other. Vicki remained still.

"Maybe Caapi will guide us tonight." Gabe sighed.

I willed for exactly this.

Krishna closed the reading. Gabe and Vicki went up to the attic to complete final tasks before the ceremony. Michael, Krishna and I moved to the couch and stared blankly at the open city.

Karon was out there somewhere, still breathing. I could just feel it.

Gabe returned to the living area half an hour later. He tried to cheer us. "Did you know scientists used to research Caapi's benefits. Now it's illegal to even talk about it. Does this make us cool or what!"

Vicki forced a laugh. Her crow-lines reminded me of Karon's. "We're only consuming what our bodies make naturally." She reassured.

They escorted us upstairs and asked us to wait outside the attic's frosted glass door. A few minutes later, Gabe chanted in a foreign language while Vicki smudged us with a strong, earthy herb called sage. After this, we were allowed in one-by-one and taken to a spot prepared especially for us.

The attic tonight looked completely different. Gym equipment was nowhere to be seen. Furniture had been moved to a corner and covered with plain, white sheets. Pot plants from Gabe's backyard were brought in and placed everywhere. The floor had five large yoga mats, one for each of us. Two cushions were on each mat. A hauntingly beautiful song played in the background. The room was lit only by candles. There was no reflective surface around; not even a single spoon in the kitchenette area.

Gabe placed an empty bucket next to each of us. "I'll lead the ceremony. Vicki will be my helper. Please throw up if you need to; don't hold back. Use the bucket. Laugh, cry, scream or dance, do what feels right. Icaros, the spirit songs, will play for rest of the evening to protect our soul as it travels in and out of our body."

Vicki filled the room with the smoke of sage. "Bathroom's to your right. If you need to use it, please raise your hand and I'll take you there. I'll also clean up any mess afterwards."

Were they being over-the-top?

Gabe pulled out a broom made of leaves from a nearby cupboard and placed it on his mat. Was it to beat us in our delirium or to attack the alleged evil spirits that come out?

Vicki handed him a bottle filled with dark, muddy liquid. Gabe poured a few drops in a lowball glass and took a sip. Vicki took one too after him. Gabe rinsed the glass out and refilled it to the brim. He went up to Krishna and signalled him to drink from it.

The corner of my eye told me Krishna struggled through his sips. When he finally finished, Gabe rinsed the glass out again. Vicki stayed behind and held Krishna's hands.

Gabe refilled the glass and came over to me. Bitterness of the brew cut through earthiness of the sage and made my nostrils twitch. I looked at the frosted door. It was closed. Gabe smiled and handed me the glass. I took a hesitant sip and tasted coffee, salt, honey and tart all at once. I got up to spit it out but he urged me to swallow. A few unpleasant moments later, I gulped the whole glass and washed it down with water. Vicki came and held my hands while Gabe moved onto Michael.

For the first fourty-five minutes, nothing happened. All I did was yawn in the setting of cushions and candles. Michael and Krishna were sitting up and resting against the wall. I laid down for a nap. Vicki came over and covered me with a blanket. The Icaros continued to play in the background.

This was too easy. Why had I been worrying?

I drifted off. Suddenly, a wave entered my stomach and turned into a churn. I sat up with a clammy forehead and shaking hands. Vicki took slow steps towards me and handed me a bucket. The Icaros turned to full blast. I let out a howl and without wanting to, without even needing to, threw up!

A black goo with mucus came out of my empty stomach. Vicki helped me to rinse my mouth out and lean against the wall behind. I held a cushion against my trembling belly. Krishna and Michael were underneath their blankets. Gabe was at a distance, and had changed out of his jeans and into a loose pyjama set.

I let out another cry. My stomach was about to escape from my mouth! Vicki was next to me in a flash and whispered, "It's okay."

"I-I need to use the b-bathroom."

She held my shoulders as we walked for a whole ten minutes to get to the bathroom next door. The volume of Icaros kept fluctuating from low to blasting. Gabe was with Michael; he was spewing in a bucket. Krishna was curled up and observing everything with a triangle of three glowing balls.

The bathroom had a shower, a toilet seat, a wash basin and a lit tea-candle. The mirror had been taken out. Even the metallic towel railing was covered with paper. I crumbled on the floor with a stomach that was squeezing and contracting. I waited for more toxins to leave my body but nothing happened. I got up and splashed some water on my face.

We walked back to the attic but took a wrong turn and instead, ended up in a deep, green forest. Olive and yellow vines ran through the ground. I was careful not to step on their fragile leaves. Vicki, who had changed into a leopard skin dress, put me under a large tree with heart-shaped leaves. "Count from ten to one."

Someone was humming at a distance. "Cassandra, Cassandra." I heard my name but was too weak to move.

The tree dropped figs into my lap. I began a feeble countdown. "Ten, nine, eight..." As soon as I said, "one," Mitten jumped out of that tree and into my arms. "Mommy I love you. Please take better care of yourself," her eyes said. I held her and cried.

My life rewound like a reel. Everything played backwards until a door appeared. I became eight once again. My mother had just refused to serve me dinner. I was walking back to my room with a growling stomach when a four-year old Jacob called out for me. He was wearing blue pyjamas with small, white stars. He was holding a carriage and mimicked its choo-choo. I ran to hug him. But he morphed into a twenty-three-year-old organic and pushed me away.

My lungs ran out of air and forgot how to pull

more in. Drip, drip, drip. Crimson droplets fell on my feet. I looked up. The sky was raining blood. My hands reached to cover my face but instead, morphed into heart-shaped leaves and flew away. I ran after them but stopped at the sight of a twelve-year-old-girl with pigtails sitting on a park bench a few meters away.

She wore a blue dress that had patterns of swirls and spirals. She was playing with a tattered teddy bear. As soon as she saw me, she got up and walked towards me. Her bloodshot eyes pierced into mine. Crimson streams flowed out of them. She handed me her bear and said, "Goodbye."

Her throbbing veins came to surface and revealed a green tar running through them. I tasted that poison in my mouth and threw up again. Vicki handed me a bucket. Icaros were back. Gabe said something incoherent. Krishna's head was down. Michael was nowhere to be seen.

"Water, please." I begged.

Vicki handed me a soft, delicious splash. I gulped it down immediately. She blew the smoke of sage on me and offered me another serve of the muddy Caapi.

"I can't." I cried.

"Just a little. You're so close to a breakthrough," she said.

I mustered enough strength and took a few more sips. Michael came back to his mat with red, swollen eyes. Vicki left to attend to him. Gabe came over in a flowing, green kurta and brushed me with a leafy broom while chanting something.

All the plants in that room came to life. Each of their leaves grew an eye. A count of hundred or more stared directly at me. I shivered and pulled my pale dress in. I swept the stray strands of hair away from my face. I straightened my back so I could appear to be in control.

The background music picked up pace. Every eye blinked to its beat. My own eyes joined their rhythm. Soon, we were in sync as one.

Soil inside the plants levitated and morphed into a mini tornado. It came towards me with a whirl. I hid my face in my elbow. Within seconds, that gush became calm. I became calm.

I opened my eyes. Dust had turned into a swirl of nanos. I was its centre. I touched one particle with my finger. Someone whispered, "For the nanochip to be a success, you need to think harder than ever. But the more you will focus on it, the more you will fail."

Could this be more contradictory?

A wormhole appeared. I got pulled deeper and deeper despite my best fight with its current. The motion sickness made me throw up. Someone handed me a bucket and rubbed my back.

Frankincense immersed the air. I could finally open my eyes. Clear quartz and black obsidians were floating in air and touching the dome of the roof above. To my right was a large, circular window. A snippet of the night sky was peeking through it, revealing a total of fourteen moons, some full and others crescent. An ocean was roaring outside, calling my name. "Cassandra! Cassandra!"

I wanted to swim in that ocean. But I also knew it was not my time yet...

I burst into tears and cried for as long as I needed to.

After I wiped my face, the wormhole reappeared and sucked me back in. Once again, I tried to fight. But the current was too strong against my drifting self.

I fell through the roof of the attic and landed on my mat.

Gabe came over as soon as I opened my eyes.

"You were gone a while!"

I looked around. Everything was exactly as I had left it a few hours ago. What had my mind just concocted?!

Vicki helped me to the bathroom. I washed my face and rinsed my mouth out. A few steps later, I joined the gathering of everyone sitting around a large oil heater.

"I couldn't stop crying and throwing up," Michael said. Krishna and I nodded at the familiarity of that experience.

"How many times did you guys change your clothes?" I asked Vicki, who was back in her maxi dress; and Gabe, who was back in his jeans.

"Not once." Gabe winked.

It was 0315 hours. We shared our visions and insights while nibbling on a platter of bananas, grapes and apples. Once we were fully back, we tried to pull together pieces of our visions to solve the jigsaw of where Karon was. But it was to no avail.

There was a long pause. Finally, Krishna spoke. "I need to leave and start a community far away. Cassandra, you'll come looking for it one day,"

This took me by complete surprise! Before I could say a word, Gabe jumped in as if he was half-expecting to hear this. "If that's what Caapi showed you, be open to change. But don't just pack your bags and disappear tomorrow."

Krishna's eyes became moist.

It was pitch-black outside. The night was still in its darkest hour.

It had taken me a lifetime to belong somewhere. The thought of us getting separated at a time when we needed each other the most unnerved me.

To push Krishna's words out of my mind, I changed the topic. "What about those who can't take Caapi for health reasons?"

"Opening ourselves up with psychedelics is a risk even for the healthiest of us. Vicki and I, along with one of our friends, did a lot of work behind the scenes to make sure tonight is safe. Regular dreaming exercises and meditation can be just as powerful in stimulating DMT."

"But all this is a waste if we don't deal with our baggage. Pain is our greatest teacher, except for when it gets out of control. Because then it eats us from within and becomes our doom. And that's what shadows feed on." Vicki added.

Icaros were playing in the background as a distant reminder of the hidden worlds we had just visited. Flashes of light were dancing in the room. For some strange reason, they were visible only to me. Suddenly, everything made sense!

"The soul grid!" I screamed.

Everyone turned towards me and asked in unison, "What?"

"In my vision quest, I heard 'for the nanochip to be a success, you need to think harder than ever. But the more you will focus on it, the more you will fail.'"

"Ohhh that is a trip!" Michael laughed.

"Right? But let's think about it. Yes, we need to get the chip right so we can become as fast as machines. But more importantly, instead of obsessing over an artificial intelligence grid, us humans need to come together and build our own grid. A grid where our hearts and souls connect us as one!" I had a sudden surge of energy as I spoke.

Faint rays broke the cover of the night and entered through the attic window. Within minutes, the dark sky turned to shades of yellow and orange.

"The soul grid! I like it." Gabe smiled.

We looked at each other and did not need to say another word.

Chapter 14 – The Devil

It was early hours of Saturday morning. We had just finished the Caapi ceremony. One by one, everyone took a cab home. I was about to order mine. But Gabe asked me to stay behind. He wanted to talk more about the soul grid.

I washed my face and brushed my teeth to freshen up. When I was back in the living room, he pressed buttons of his coffee machine. A wheezing and swishing later, steam escaped from its nozzle and filled the mugs underneath with creamy cappuccino. "The soul grid sounds promising." He brought the coffees to the couch.

I nodded. "Connecting through love and forgiveness. Standing together as one. Maybe that's the only grid strong enough to override artificial intelligence and break the control we're under."

"Do you think us humans are capable of putting our differences aside?" He asked a rhetorical question.

I let out a pessimistic laugh. "Not everyone can but as long as we have majority votes. Getting fifty-one percent on our side should be easy enough, right?"

He joined my sad laughter. "Virtual reality…AI…has taken over our minds, regardless of whether we're chipped or not. And media is wielding it like a sword. In a way, this is a psychedelic too…influencing us, showing us only what it wants to."

I took a sip and contemplated the uncanny truth in his words.

He continued. "You know about atom bomb, right? Oppenheimer made it to protect his country. Einstein supported it coz he didn't want the Nazis to win. But the bomb destroyed Japan and traumatised the rest of the world."

"I wonder how the early AI and microchip scientists would feel about their inventions today? What if my nanochip wreaks havoc too? That's why I can't just leave my job. I need to stay to help make better choices."

There was an uncomfortable, contemplative pause.

"By the way, I saw that homeless lady, Cynthia, the other day." I broke the ice.

"Oh good! I was getting worried."

"She said something about a scene being set and how it was time to act."

Gabe laughed. "Sounds about right! I met her a few years ago when I was depressed. It triggered a chain of events, and here I am, dreaming."

I did not know what to make of it. "She has delusions of persecution. Normal people don't act like her."

"True. But maybe coz of her instability, the psychedelic of virtual reality has no hold on her. And maybe, just maybe, she can see things you and I can't."

"According to her, demons are after me." I picked at the dry cuticles around my fingernails.

"What do you think?"

Yeah… What exactly did I think?

My nerves made me change the topic to ADAM. I gave Gabe a quick snapshot of me breaking into his apartment in search of answers and coming across his diary.

Gabe's expression did not give much away.

I continued to talk. "One thing's been bugging me. ADAM's last entry said if he died, it'll not be an accident or a suicide but a murder!"

A concerned look clouded Gabe's face. He took a few sips of his coffee. "Then again, he hadn't been himself since his daughter JOSIE got taken away."

"But JOSIE's dead! ADAM wrote so in his diary."

"JOSIE'S alive! The Family Branch took her away coz they deemed him an unfit parent. He fought hard but lost. His wife didn't want her custody, so the poor thing ended up in an orphanage."

"Then why did ADAM say she's dead?"

"Dunno. Maybe he told RYAN but he's gone too…"

"Speaking of RYAN…He ran into me one night and gave me a piece of paper with a microchip barcode written on it."

"Goodness Cassandra! You really were entangled with us long before you joined us."

"Or maybe I joined coz I was entangled? Chicken n egg…"

Gabe let out a laugh. "RYAN was a drifter. Very calculated though. If he gave you a message, he would've had his reasons."

It was nearly 0600 hours. I finished my coffee and thanked Gabe. He went to call me a cab, but I decided to walk instead to clear my head.

"Call me straight away if something happens," he said as I left the cocoon of his home.

My first step out was met with distant barking of a neighbour's dog. I wondered how Mitten had slept through the night and if she was meowing in Divine's ears right about now?

A few minutes later, I reached the main road. Horns were shrieking. Their frustration unleashed a migraine in me. I changed my route and turned into a side street. A night club had just closed its doors. Scantily dressed women in high heels crowded the front and leaned on arms of wavering men. The air reeked of alcohol, cigarettes and urine. I lowered my head and quickened my pace, wishing to be back with the horns. My shoulder bumped into that of a man who was barely twenty. His agitated, grey eyes charged at me. He expected me to flinch, but his anger did not scare me; instead, his pain caused a knot in my throat. He opened his mouth to say something foul but retreated at the last minute. It was as if he knew I had seen his broken self through his tough façade.

I continued to walk. Strong sunrays streaked through the fog and offered me their warmth. The City clock chimed a half-past.

A dog came out of nowhere and stood in front of me. I knelt and gave him a pat. But his big, brown eyes wanted something else. He barked, walked away, looked back at me and barked again. I took his cue and followed him for twenty minutes. He led me to a narrow alley, which opened into a carpark. At the other end was a large pillar, which marked the beginning of the Harbour Bridge. The suburban half of the city with picket fences and regular Family Branch visits was on the other side.

We walked to a small, green area underneath the bridge where dirty mattresses and sleeping bags were laid on the ground. People were tossing and turning on them. It reminded me of the mats we were on just a few hours ago. But instead of being filled with earthy herbs that offered protection, this air was stale and weighed heavy. Also, there were no life-giving plants promising support; only overflowing garbage bags piled up in trolleys.

No Gabe or Vicki were here to comfort these poor souls. What unfortunate vision quest were they on?

"Oi Jimmy! Com' ea boi." A raspy voice screamed.

The dog left my side and ran towards a woman who sat ten metres way. Her fragile head was swallowed by a black, tattered beanie, which came all the way down to her eyes and hung loosely around her ears. Jimmy curled up next to her. She patted him with her tiny hands that were tucked inside a pair of oversize gloves. He barked. She reached into a bag next to her and pulled out an old, dry bone. He grabbed it between his teeth and chewed on it.

Other people under this bridge were waking up and mumbling morning sounds. The pillar's shadow was keeping their sun away; the same sun that had me fully drenched. I stood there like a voyeur mushroom. No one noticed me. Was I that invisible? Or that irrelevant?

Jimmy barked again.

"Shut up or I'll kick ya!" An aged man on a mattress next to her screamed.

"Don't yell at ma Jimmy! Hez a good boi." The woman fought back.

The man grunted and curled back in his blanket.

Jimmy leaned in closer to her. She hugged him.

I walked up to her, perhaps because Caapi was still circulating through my system and giving me courage. As soon as I saw her piercing green eyes, I recognised her! I wondered if she remembered me too...?

"Hi, I'm Cassandra." I extended my hand out instinctively, then pulled it back immediately.

"World endin'....people dyin'. I'm gonna save 'em all." She swatted invisible flies away from around her face.

I smiled. "When is this world not ending?"

"Mark of the beast got us...'em demons are comin'. We gotta fight back." She mumbled and scratched her arms.

Gabe and Krishna's words rang in my ears and unnerved me. Was Cynthia talking in a metaphor or could she see something I could not?

Jimmy finished chewing on his dry bone and placed it on the bag it came out of. It was too much precision for a stray dog. Cynthia wrapped it in a rag and put it back in that bag. It was too much thought for a fragmented mind.

The knot in my throat tightened, only this time, with water in my eyes. "Hi, I'm Cassandra." I reintroduced myself.

"Loud, scary faces...I hid in dumpster...Jimmy ma boi found ma..." Cynthia mumbled about the day when I had left work humiliated after getting reported to the Grid. Hearing her version of events embarrassed me. Had I really charged at a poor, unstable woman? At least this made her find Jimmy, so some good came out of it.

My eyes looked at the ground. She laid back on the damp mattress claiming her six feet of it.

I went up to a local café and bought eight large take-away breakfasts, coffees and bottles of water for everyone. Also, I went to the grocers nearby and bought a bag of dog food and a bone. Once I delivered these, I took Cynthia's hands in mine. Her eyes flashed an understanding.

"I can't leave Jimmy alone. Not when demons are coming." This time, she spoke with an eloquence I had not seen in her before. It alarmed and comforted me both. I added her name to my list right after RYAN's, and without saying another word, walked away.

Why were these bizzare moments pulling me into Cynthia's schizophrenic world over and over again? The first time we had crossed paths, I ran away from her and found Krishna and the Dreaming group, which opened my life. The second time we had crossed paths, she ran from me and found Jimmy, who was patiently sitting next to her. I prayed the love of this animal would save her soul.

Maybe there *is* a fine line between insanity and divinity after-all. And I had been treading it all along...

Lost in my thoughts, I did not even realise when my feet carried me home. When I opened my apartment door, Divine was pacing up and down the living room. She sighed as soon as she saw me. "Cassandra just walked in," she said out loud.

Muffled words echoed. She handed me her phone. "Gabe wants to talk to you."

Even before I could say a hello, Gabe launched into me. "Good God Cassandra! We were worried sick.

You didn't even answer our calls!"

I pulled my phone out of my handbag and saw a stream of notifications from both Gabe and Divine.

"Sorry...my phone was on silent...and I ran into Cynthia..."

"Have you seen the news? A woman from your work has died! And Karon's still missing. We need to be more careful!"

Divine pulled up the NewsLink site. It read:

A 31-year-old scientist commits suicide to 'escape hallucinations'

Dr Sara Berry, 31, had been complaining of 'dark shadows' for the last four months, her partner Mr HARRY RUDD reported. They moved houses three months ago on Dr Berry's insistence. But she said the 'shadows' followed her into their new home. This morning in a depressive episode, Ms Berry overdosed on a toxic cocktail and passed away.

Mr RUDD reported he never saw anything strange in their home.

Dr Berry had no history of psychiatric illness. However, she had stopped taking stabilisers five months prior.

This is the sixth such report in four months. Please contact your local health professional immediately if you or anyone you know is struggling with an imbalance.

I stared at the screen. No matter how hard I tried, no words came out. Sara, my fellow scientist, had moved houses because of shadows...? The same shadows that were haunting me...?

My mind flashed back to a breadcrumb moment that made all the sense in this hindsight. 'That's five people now....' She had whispered over coffee months ago when we were talking about ADAM burning his apartment down. I wish I had said something... anything...instead of remaining quiet and running home straight after.

Divine hugged my numb frame and asked me to breathe.

"We need to get Cynthia off from streets! I can help!!" I trembled.

"Get some sleep. We'll talk later." Gabe hung up.

Divine offered to make breakfast. However, I was not hungry. Also, I wanted to be left alone. She kissed me goodbye and said, "Sleep tight."

But how could I?

That evening, I was meeting Steven to discuss 'the glitch' in his experiments and, if things went well, decode the mystery behind RYAN's piece of paper. But after hearing of Sara's passing, I wanted to cancel our plans and curl up on my bed. Gabe and I already knew there was more to ADAM's alleged suicide. Could Sara's be a foul play too?

I kept sinking deeper into my thoughts. Steven called and snapped me out. 'I just saw her last week! She even told us the chip will be ready soon."

"She was in that meeting with PROF AMON, DR HEATH and you?"

"Yeah. DEE and I asked where you were, but PROF AMON said you had a clash with another meeting. You didn't know?"

"No…!"

Did Sara betray me as well?

There was a long pause. Steven cleared his throat and said, "It's okay if you want to cancel tonight."

The show needed to go on, and now more than ever. I straightened my spine and said, "Thanks, but I'll see you at seven."

"Come to the Grid's headquarters. I'm based there while DEE's away."

After Steven's call, I managed a few hours of broken sleep. When I woke up, Mitten was next to me, licking herself. I kissed her forehead. She meowed and kneaded me with her soft paws.

I drank a cup of strong coffee and jumped into a hot shower. I brushed my teeth and scrubbed my hair. I cleaned under my nails and behind my ears. Karon's missing and Sara's death had shaken me. These had also strengthened me. I was not going to be next in line at the slaughterhouse.

I dried myself and put on a red and a black bohemian dress that ended just above my knees. I wrapped a grey coat around it and wore black, ankle-length boots. My make-up was some concealer and a pink lip-gloss. I combed through my long, dark hair and left it to settle in natural waves. Just before leaving home, I dabbed some serum in it.

A short cab-ride later, I was back at the Grid's headquarters. The grey frame with the wall of moss brought back the last time I was here, which was to provide information about my encounter with RYAN. Agent FIELD had screamed, "consider this your first and final warning!" Agent JOHNSTON had softened the blow. "We have high hopes from you." They had even convinced me to remain on their team. But in that fateful moment, Karon's message had popped up on my screen. *I will be at the New Green Centre 224 at 1:30 pm this Saturday. If you are still interested, please turn up.* And I did…

Steven was waiting outside the main entrance. "You know, you do that a lot."

"Do what?"

"Disappearing into your own little world."

Huh! Guess some things never change.

Steven was wearing a crisp, silver-grey collared shirt with dark pants. He had messy hair and a three-day shadow on his face. He smelt of citrus and reminded me of spring. I was glad I had picked one of my better dresses to wear and paired it with a natural look.

A Juli.R was "sleeping" at the counter, or in other words, rebooting itself. We walked past the main lifts. Steven took us around the corner and opened a small storage closet with his access key. To my surprise, it led us to a dimly lit corridor that had a large lift, which was hidden from the public view. When we got in, Steven pressed floor number five.

My eyes widened.

"I was the same when DEE first brought me here." He laughed.

"I thought the underground floors were just an urban myth! Are they hiding aliens here?"

"No, just other weird stuff." He winked.

The lift stopped on the fifth floor and opened to reveal a lobby that was filled with colourful pot plants leaning against walls of monochrome purple. We entered a lab area, which was a giant hall divided into several rooms. Each room was set up with a bed and monitoring devices. "For sleep studies." Steven said.

We walked to his office that had one large and two standard screens. "To review MRI scans and data files." He added.

"This lab is so different from Servitium! In fact, from any other lab I've seen."

"Lemme show you something else." He logged onto his computer. An application popped up. He entered his password. A message appeared: *System Error 14262105.*

"See that...?" He turned to me.

"Yeah....? An awfully long error code...?"

"Just wait..."

Steven leaned into me. His arm brushed against mine. His hand rested on my shoulder. "Five...four...three...two..." He counted under his breath. A blue-black screensaver appeared as soon as he said, "one." A second later, another message popped up, which read: *Scanning.* He looked at me with raised brows. Did he expect me to say something?

Suddenly, that screensaver whirled like a tornado and morphed into a gaunt face with hollow eyes! Before I knew, it leapt out of the monitor!!

"I am coming for you!" It screeched and went straight through me.

I flinched back and lost my balance. The face disintegrated into thin air right before my eyes. Steven took me in his arms and stopped me from hitting the floor.

It was the same face that had been haunting my home!!! Had Steven seen it too or was I hallucinating again?

A message appeared on the screen: *Cassandra, they are here for you.*

Another message appeared immediately after: *Run and hide.*

"Is this a sick joke?" I pushed Steven away.

"It's this bloody software! It says the creepiest things to me too. It even knows details from my childhood. Stuff I had long forgotten.... stuff I had told no-one!"

Steven's words hit me hard. Even I had told no-one, not a single soul, about the gaunt face and what it had said to me.

Suddenly, Cynthia's words screamed in my mind. 'Them demons are comin'!'

My head was spinning. My hands were trembling. I sat down. Steven brought me a bottle of water from a fridge nearby. I opened the cap and took a sip.

"Why exactly did you bring me here?"

"Coz it's important! I tried to tell DEE but she asked me keep my mouth shut. The next day, she upgraded my contract and promised I'll be on cover of the Global."

Global was the top-most scientific journal in which only the best minds of our time appeared. "It's my dream to have just one miserly paper published in it. To be on its cover is like being a rock star!"

"I wasn't promised this on merit, Cassandra! DEE's treating me like a pawn...a mindless pawn. My entire career, a whole decade of hard work, is on the line."

"Why are you telling me this?"

"Coz I know I can trust you."

My head was still spinning.

Steven spoke without taking a breath. "This started a few weeks ago when I was working late. The software launched on its own and typed, 'I know.' I thought someone was pranking me. Then messages appeared on the screen. Stuff from my life...stuff I had been thinking that very day...! It was as if someone was inside my head...reading my mind! I grabbed my bag and ran out. Then a shadow came at me. It went right through me and disappeared!"

Shadow? My ears perked up. I opened my mouth to share my own experiences, but Steven continued to talk. "This software, program, app, whatever it is…. it's just a messenger. Lemme show you the computer that's feeding it." He grabbed my arm and took me to another room a few doors down.

As soon as he unlocked that room, automated lights came on to reveal a small, oval, holographic door in the middle. Countless tubes and wires were running through it.

My jaw dropped at the out-worldly, golden hue it emitted. "What is it?" I whispered.

"A quantum computer."

"A quantum what…?!"

"A quantum computer. It mines information on Earth, information about us, to look at patterns. The Grid's using it to calculate every possible future. Somehow, and I don't know how, but it can also predict the past!"

I sank into the wall behind and stared at the hologram, which was circling anti-clockwise and making a dull hum. Streams of light were dancing in and around its tubes and wires.

"Steven, I don't understand this at all! It's waaay above my pay-grade."

"You think I do? I brought you here coz it told me weeks ago Sara would die. I checked in with her to make sure she was okay. She seemed fine. Next thing, she killed herself! Can you imagine how I feel?"

Yes, I could.

While we were talking, a tall and lanky humanoid figure appeared in the far corner of the room. Hair at the back of my neck stood up at the sight of its glowing, red eyes. A sharp pain went through my heart. My head became light. I was pulled into another world, one where a little girl came running towards me with blood shot eyes. My knees became soft----

NO!!! NO!!! NOOOOO!!!

I could not go back there! Not now, not ever! 'I will myself to be safe and protected. I will myself to be safe and protected.' I closed my eyes and screamed in my mind.

Steven paused for a moment, then continued. "It told me after Sara dies, the course will be set. You'll be next. Then me."

So, I really was in line at the slaughterhouse…? How much bad news could one day bring?

"This quantum computer, is it evil?" I asked.

"Dunno. It just spits out information."

"Why is it telling us stuff?" I took a step towards Steven.

"Dunno." He took a step towards me.

The shadow took a small, silent step towards us both. It was as if it knew we knew.

I looked at Steven and signalled at the door with my eyes. "I gotta tell you, this whole thing's very weird. I really don't understand it."

"You think I do?" He repeated.

He grabbed my hand. Together, we ran out and closed the door behind. We did not stop until we got to his office and turned all the lights on.

A message was waiting for us on the screen. It read: RYAN ANGELO. INC0418402.

Chapter 15 – The Tower

RYAN ANGELO. INC0418402.

My eyes shot out of their sockets.

The message disappeared a moment later, giving us control of the screen back. Steven logged onto the Dream Catcher study database, and frantically clicked the dashboard here and there. After a couple of minutes, he said, "This barcode belongs to one of the participants. But he's dead."

My breath stopped midway. That it was RYAN's barcode came as no surprise to me. But what significance did it have?

"Tell me more…?" I asked.

"There isn't much more to tell. We recruited ANGELO through the University. I met him a few times and handed him over to my research assistant Juli.R for data collection. One day he got murdered. As per our protocol, Juli.R archived his file."

"What protocol?"

"We only analyse data of participants who remain with us till the end. Otherwise, it skews results. When ANGELO was murdered, Julie.R excluded his file with this note here: the subject is no longer in the study due to his untimely demise."

We quickly scanned the file. A dark blue notification caught my attention. RYAN had sent an email a few hours before he was murdered. "It's unread!" I shrieked.

Steven opened the message and read it out loud. "I'm dreaming again. Real dreams! Sometimes I even know I'm in one! But I'm scared coz I'm being followed. Can I speak to Dr Wilson? It's urgent."

We stared at the screen for a very long minute and did not blink once. RYAN had truncated his words. Organics never did that because both their verbal and written vocabulary was polished by AI.

"Steven?" I nudged.

He dropped his head into his hands and pulled on his hair. "I never got this message. I was at a conference in Copenhagen. By the time I got back, ANGELO had been murdered. And that numbskull robot had already archived his file."

Did this mean.... could it be that.... that RYAN came looking for me because he had tried to contact Steven but failed...?

"I saw him just before he was murdered." I relayed the evening when he dragged me under a jacaranda tree and forced his barcode details in my hands.

Steven looked at me with shocked eyes. In the eerie silence of that haunted basement, I could hear my heartbeat, and in fact, his too.

"I'm gonna download his file and dissect it tonight." He finally managed a few words.

"Let's review it together. I'll make coffee." I wanted to get to the bottom of this myself.

After Steven finished the download, we quickly packed up and turned the lights off. I was nervous about lurking shadows and kept my thumb on the torch button of my phone. But there were no more incidents. We managed to walk out of the building without drawing unnecessary attention to ourselves.

Our cab arrived as soon as we got to the ground floor. Within minutes, we were outside my apartment building.

When we exited the lift on my level, loud rap music confronted our ears.

"Arrr...! Since the new neighbours moved in, it's one loud party after another." I sighed.

"Maybe it's a good thing...? Too many witnesses for anyone to try hurt you."

"Uh! Or maybe it's created so much foot-traffic anyone can come and go as they please."

The party was spilled out into the corridor. Just as I was about to open the door of my apartment, one of the twins waved. She was wearing a shimmering backless dress with zirconia studded stilettos. I could not see whether this twin had a mole near her left eyebrow or not.

"Cassandra! Cassandra's date! Come join us!" She came closer.

It was PEARL.

"My date?" I repeated.

Steven's cheeks became flushed.

I opened my mouth to make an excuse. But PEARL interjected. "You never come over!"

I smiled and said something non-committal. She did have a point though. The twins always dropped an invite under my door. It was me who needed to reciprocate. But tonight was not the night to start.

I opened my apartment door. Mitten was waiting for us. I picked her up. She yawned. I gave her a kiss and put her back on the floor.

"Let's drop by for a drink. You need to make friends around here in case something happens,"

Steven said.

We put our coats and bags on the dining table. After I topped up Mitten's bowl, we made our way to PEARL and JADE's.

This was the first time I had been inside that apartment since it became theirs. The living room walls did not have exotic landscapes anymore; instead, they were covered with professional photographs of the twins in bikinis. Where used to be Richard and Laura's bookshelf was now a black-and-white painting of a naked woman. Chess and Scrabble board-games on the centre-table were replaced by a phallic-shaped vase with plastic flowers.

I recognised many faces from our building including the ones I had never spoken to in my five years there.

Alcohol flowed freely. A tray with a pile of white powder was in the centre, with lines surrounded it. A robot offered us drinks. Steven grabbed a beer. I opted for a glass of white wine.

I was envious of how carefree the twins were. It was as if they had no worry in the world.

"Finaaallly!" JADE, who wreaked of alcohol, stumbled up to us. She was wearing a maroon lace top with a dark mini skirt and had matching heels on.

PEARL leaned in and supported her. I smiled and introduced Steven for the first time.

"Dat creepy wuman….! Beady eyes…no braaows. Tell er to stop annoyin' us..." She barely managed to finish her sentence before crashing on the couch.

"I better take her to the bedroom." PEARL picked JADE up from her left side. Steven helped from her right. As we were walking down the corridor, I asked, "What was JADE talking about?"

"You do not know?! This weird looking woman, about five foot, has been fishing information about you for weeks. She even tried to befriend us," PEARL said.

Beady eyes? No brows? Five foot? Only CHANDRIANA matched that description. But what did she want from me? Sara had been dealing with her.

"She's been here?" I was in disbelief. The sick feeling in my stomach returned.

"A few weeks ago, we caught her trying to break into your apartment. She said you had asked her to house-sit, but she had misplaced the keys. Of course, we did not believe her and reported her straight-away. I am surprised the cops did not call you to get your side of the story!"

What was CHANDRIANA up to? And why did the cops not contact me?

We laid JADE down on her bed and took her stilettos off. She twitched slightly, then rolled over and let out a snore.

I felt guilty for judging the two thoughtful books by their socialite covers. "Thanks for looking out for me," I said.

PEARL smiled. JADE continued to snore.

"You have a beautiful home, by the way. I'm sorry I haven't been here before. You'll need help cleaning up for sure. I'm free tomorrow."

PEARL laughed. "Thank you darling, but I am ordering robots."

"Well, take my number, just in case. Steven and I need to leave soon; we have work to do. But let's have lunch sometime next week."

After we exchanged phone numbers, PEARL

saw us to the door.

A few seconds later, we were back in my apartment. Rap beats from the party followed us. But today, the loud music was not as annoying.

Steven and I washed our hands. I put some frozen potato pastry puffs in the oven, made some plunger coffee and laid out a platter of olives, crackers and macadamia cheese on the dining table.

While I was prepping, Steven told me he was an only child. He showed an aptitude for mathematics and sciences from an early age. Therefore, he entered the profession of his choice, which was medicine. During his training, he developed an interest in life beyond death and became a research scientist in cryonics. Soon after, the opportunity to lead the Dream Catcher study landed in his lap.

It sounded way too planned. The Grid would not have had it any other way.

I told him a little about myself but skimped on details relating to my family.

Steven turned on his laptop and got to work. "ANGELO. Age, thirty-one; profession, stockbroker; reason for opting into the study, self-improvement."

"Pretty standard stuff."

Twenty minutes later, the pastry puffs were ready. I took them out of the oven and brought them over. We sipped our coffees and nibbled on bites while Steven continued to click. His eyes narrowed as soon as he saw a sub-folder three levels down from the main. It was marked *confidential.*

"I've never seen this before!" He tried some passwords that did not work. He chewed on his nails restlessly, looked up some trouble-shooting tips online, did some resets and half an hour later, was finally able to open that sub-folder.

"These are progress notes from Juli.R! The first one, dated November last year, says, *the subject reported having a dream last night. But he is unsure if it was a natural or a Dream Catcher download.*"

"English please."

"There are two types of dreams. The first are natural, which are banned and basically, impossible to have nowadays. The second are the AI ones form our study, which come from our test catalogue filled with desirable experiences that one can download during sleep. It seems ANGELO did have a dream soon after enrolling with us but could not determine if it was a natural or a catalogued."

I ate a spicy puff while trying to keep up. But the loud music from next door kept breaking my focus.

Steven kept us on track. "The second entry is from January this year. It documents, *the subject reports a spike in dreaming activity and states he has them every night. He describes a dream in which someone is urging him to stop taking stabilisers.*"

My mind instantly came into focus.

"We for sure did not put that message in the catalogue!" Steven said.

We looked at each other and laughed hysterically. It was better than panicking.

When we calmed down, I leaned over and read another entry. "The subject, an organic, is booked for an in-depth examination to determine how he is accessing natural dreams."

"Juli.R didn't flag this with me. It's not even mentioned in any of the formal reports."

"So…Juli.R was running its own show?"

Steven nodded. "Based on instructions from

whoever programmed it in the first place, which was DEE."

We took a deep breath.

There was one final note, which was dated February 2060. It read: *the subject is no longer involved in the study due to his untimely death.*

Steven clamped his fists and scrunched his face. "Arr...!" He let his frustration out.

This made me reflect on my situation. I would be lying if I said I was in full control of my own nanochip study.

There was a long pause while the penny dropped even more.

"You think there's a connection between cryonics and dreaming? Is this why DEE headhunted me?" Steven broke the silence.

"Dunno. But it seems that weird computer in the Grid's basement is warning us. Does this mean it's good?"

"I was thinking about that. When it was built, its predominant code was to protect us humans. Maybe it's just following that programming...?"

Before we could discuss this further, my phone rang. Gabe's name flashed on the screen. This late? It was either a very good or a very bad news. My stomach sank immediately.

I picked up the encrypted call without wanting to.

As soon as I said, "hello," Gabe's teary voice pierced me.

"The Crime Branch called. Karon's body was found in an abandoned warehouse not far from here."

Everything froze except for his voice at the other end.

"They're still investigating. All we know is, she was poisoned a few days after getting kidnapped."

I sank into the couch. My Caapi vision quest flashed before my eyes. It had shown me green poison running through the veins of a young girl. I had thought she was me. Perhaps it was Karon. Or was it the both of us...?

I could hear Gabe trying to hold back tears. He took a breath and said, "I have a friend who's an informer. He has some information and will be at our meeting tomorrow."

I managed my own words after a long pause. "Can I bring a friend too? We've stumbled on something unusual."

"What is it?"

"It's a...a lot to tell over the phone."

"Do you trust your friend?"

"Completely."

"Then we'll see him tomorrow. Stay safe."

I ended the call.

Steven came up to me. "She's gone, isn't she?"

A tear left my eye. Soon, it turned into two streams. That was answer enough. The clock ticked louder than ever.

He held my hand and wiped my tears. "I'll look up ANGELO, Sara and Karon in the Global Microchip database to see what's going on."

I was doing all I could to hold myself together. "Thanks. Also, I want you to meet people who know about natural dreams and have inside information."

Steven took down details of the Dreaming group meeting. We agreed to meet an hour before the meeting at NGC 224 the next day.

After staying with me for another hour, he

called a cab, kissed my forehead and left.

I went into an autopilot mode and turned my shower on. I stripped down and stood underneath the hot water. My silent tears became loud sobs. I had known Karon for only a short while, but our friendship had grown fast. She deserved so much better! It was completely unfair!!

After an eternity, I turned the shower off and patted myself dry. I put on a cotton shirt with shorts and collapsed on the bed. Mitten jumped in soon after. Before I knew, everything turned into a restless darkness.

I barely slept that night and opened my tired eyes early the next morning. There was only a second of peace before the nightmare returned.

I stumbled out of the bed and brushed my teeth. I wanted to make a cup of coffee but had no energy to drag myself to the kitchen. Therefore, I went back to the bed to disappear under the covers.

Suddenly, a notification popped up on my phone. My heart jumped when I saw the screen. It read: *1 new email from Richard Blunt.*

This was Richard's first message since leaving the building four months ago in a rush without even saying a proper goodbye.

Chapter 16 – The Star, the Moon and the Sun

What if the stars are the children of the moon the mother and the sun the father?

Richard and Laura had woken up one day and left my life like complete strangers would. They had also disconnected their phones. I emailed them a couple of weeks after their departure, but it had gone unanswered. I then wrote another email. That also disappeared into nowhere. For four whole months, I waited to hear a word without knowing if I ever would. And just when I had let go, there was a notification: *1 new email from Richard Blunt.* This infuriated me because our connection was clearly on their terms.

Without opening that email, I put my phone on charge and left it in a corner. I washed and refilled Mitten's food and water bowls and made a strong cup of coffee. I promised myself to not read that email for at least a whole day. After-all, I had more important things to focus on.

But my resolve lasted all of ten minutes. Before I knew, I was back in my bedroom and my fingers had tapped on the dark blue message. It read:

Sorry kiddo. I could not even look you in the eyes when we left.

Please forgive Laura. She is a weak woman driven by

fear. She did not realise what she was doing. She only wanted to keep me out of trouble. But in doing so, she selfishly reported you to the Grid. I had to get her away before she caused more harm.

What?!?! It was Laura who had reported me to the Grid, not Caleb and EMMA? But what about their conversation in which they had confessed to murdering RYAN and having a plan for me too?

I sank into my bed and continued to read.

Laura and I got into another argument after we left. Our cab veered off the road and crashed into a tree. Laura, the devil's woman, is of course fine. But I ended up with multiple fractures. I was even hospitalised for a few days.

Soon after getting discharged, I developed severe pain, had problems breathing and passed out on our kitchen floor one night. I was rushed to a local hospital where we found out my body had gone into a septic shock. I'm now in a quarantine room with antibiotics pumping into my veins. Most of my organs have failed. Maybe the gods are punishing me for what Laura did to you.

I could not have died without letting you know why we left the way we did. Please forgive us, kiddo.

My head became light. Was I in a nightmare? I looked at my hands. Unfortunately, they did not change.

Did Laura even realise how her actions had destroyed my life?

I drafted a sharp response back. But my fingers could not press *send*. The last thing Richard needed was my anger. Therefore, I deleted everything and instead, wrote back:

This was not your fault. Please fight the sepsis and get better soon. I pray we will meet again.

But deep down, I knew we would never. Multiple-organ failure is not something one just recovers from. I had no choice but to face Richard, my father-figure, was dying. The worst part was, I could not even hold his hand and send him off. All I could do was sit in silence and hold a cold cup of coffee.

A few hours later, I took a quick shower and got dressed in a pair of dark jeans, a beige top and a burgundy coat. I dragged myself out of the house and made a quick stop at Mango Moksha to pick up two large quinoa salads as snacks for the Dreaming group meeting. While I was waiting for my order, my gloomy eyes looked over at the corner where Richard, Laura and I used to sit. How time changes. Then so do we…

Steven met me at NGC 224 soon after to provide an update on what he had found in the Global Microchip Database. This was the first time I had been back to the park since Karon and I ran its circumference.

Steven was waiting for me by the fountain with splashing streams. He waved as soon as he saw me. We walked towards each-other. He was dressed in a dark blue collared shirt and grey pants. His hair was bedroom messy and his face had a three-day shadow. He handed me an almond cappuccino and said, "The Dream Catcher therapy somehow stimulated ANGELO'S thalamus, medial prefrontal cortex and posterior cingulate cortex to make him have actual dreams!"

"Isn't this the one thing you guys didn't want?" I could not help but laugh at the irony of the situation.

He frowned.

I retreated. "Okay, okay, sorry! How did this happen?"

We found a soft patch of grass in a quiet corner and turned our phones off.

"Growing up, ANGELO had an attention deficit disorder. On his fourteenth birthday, his parents got him microchipped. Soon after, he made a lot of currency in trading. There was even a position waiting for him in the Grid. At twenty-six, he had a car accident and ended up in a coma. When he recovered, he made changes to his life and enrolled into my Dream Catcher study."

"Hmmm…that would be around the time he joined the Dreaming group as well. Gabe told me he was a loner. But his social media showed him as outgoing."

"I think something happened to him when he was in a coma. I'm not sure what, though. But it made our study protocol stimulate his brain to activate natural dreams. Juli.R picked up on it and bypassed me to put an alert on his profile."

"Does this mean he was murdered coz he could dream?"

"Not sure…."

"He had a friend ADAM who committed suicide. He used to dream as well. Wonder if there's a link…?"

"ADAM was mentioned in ANGELO'S file. Poor guy. Got divorced, lost his mental balance, his daughter was forced into foster care."

"JOSIE's the daughter. Is she alive still?"

"Dunno. All it said was he believed his daughter was murdered and it was a coverup."

Why was this rabbit-hole getting deeper? I tried to maintain my focus. "Anything on Sara or Karon?"

"Couldn't check. Someone came in."

It was almost time. I told Steven we needed to keep our phones off and leave them in a designated area before heading to Gabe's attic. He nodded. We took last sips of our coffees and caught a train to head to the meeting.

Once we arrived at Gabe's, he opened the door and greeted us with a warm smile. After I introduced Steven and him, he said, "Cassandra, glad you could come early. Our informer friend is here."

Our?

He disappeared. A moment later, he came back with a dark-haired man in jeans and a casual tee-shirt. "Still alive Cassandra? I was beginning to wonder!"

I darted a look of disbelief to Gabe. He reassured me. "Caleb and I've known each other for almost three years. He's the leader of the Rebellion movement and helped me to set up the Dreaming group."

The same Rebellion movement that was causing conflict between organics and seers? That demanded reclassifying dreams as normal and having surveillance removed? That Caleb himself asked me to stay away from?

"You kept this from me? Didn't you trust me?" I punched his forearm.

He flinched. "I didn't wanna put you at risk. By the way, my relationship with EMMA is just an act to get inside information."

"So, you did see me that morning! Why didn't you say something?"

"You threw up before I could! It was hilarious actually. I tried to contact you afterwards. But you didn't wanna talk. That's when I asked Gabe for help."

As hurt as I was, I was also relieved. My best

friend of years had not betrayed me. But he had kept a pretty big secret from me, even if he had a semi-valid reason.

"How did you get involved with this?" I asked.

"I put two n two together and knew something wasn't right. Then I met someone four years ago who asked me to be an agent. I didn't wanna keep it from you. But the less you knew, the safer you were."

I did not like it. But I understood it. I told Caleb about Laura's betrayal and Richard dying.

He rolled his eyes. "Never liked that Laura. Poor Richard, though."

He leaned in to hug me but stopped when he finally noticed Steven.

A guilty lump settled in my throat. "I've gotten to know Steven quite well over these last weeks. He has information that can help us."

Caleb and Steven shook awkward hands.

By that stage, others had arrived as well. We moved up to the attic. While Caleb, Steven and I were talking, Gabe, Michael and Krishna laid the table. We had my quinoa salad with pomegranate and almonds; Michael's felafel salad; Vicki's sourdough bread with hummus; and JOEL's pastries filled with sundried tomatoes and olives.

Once Steven and Caleb introduced themselves to everyone, we filled our plates and got seated.

Gabe handed the floor to Caleb, who said, "The Grid's preparing the next generation of robots. We need to tread carefully."

"What else is new?" Michael hissed.

"*We* are that next generation." Caleb shot back immediately.

"Sorry what?" Divine shrieked.

"The Grid tried its best but failed to create super-robots coz even the best ones had limitations. That's why it plans to turn all of us into biological robots by combining our human potential with a machine's abilities. It'll feed two birds with one scone. The Grid will get its mindless super-humans who'll do anything. And we'll lose our free-will and discernment, and never rebel."

I remembered the symposium EMMA was organising. *Humans plus Artificial Intelligence equals Infinite Potential.* Suddenly, it took a whole new meaning.

"We need to act now, or everyone will become an irreversible, next level organic within a couple of years." Gabe added.

My heart sank. "You're talking about the nanochip, aren't you? Caleb, why were you forcing me to work on it when I wanted to bail out a few months ago?"

Caleb sighed. "Coz back then, I didn't know this was the plan."

Steven said, "It all makes sense! People like ANGELO can block artificial stimuli and break through conditioning. That's why our Dream Catcher experiments weren't working on him. It wasn't the silicon that was the problem; it was the mind protecting its own self!"

Caleb said, "Exactly! ANGELO wasn't the only one either. This triggered the Grid's greatest fear. What if seers and organics came together and rebelled?"

My heart shattered into a million pieces. How could it not? My dedication, intelligence and ethics had been manipulated to serve a really dark agenda.

"At this point, chipped or not, whoever can *see*

is getting murdered or *suiciding*. I wish I could've helped ANGELO. But I had no idea this was going on. EMMA killed him, and actually, many more. But his murder went viral coz of his status. The Grid was forced to keep up appearances and pretend to investigate it. Cassandra, that bought you some time. But EMMA's closing in."

"Why? I'm just as much a villain as she is!" Was I not? If anything, my life's work was the centre of this whole agenda.

"No, you're not. Nanochip is just an energy. It's about how we use it. Imagine having super-human abilities with a heart of gold! But yes, if we continue sleeping, we'll go even deeper into mind control," Caleb said.

"The question isn't whether the nanochip is good or bad. The real questions are, is our morality ready for it? And even if it is, do we really need it inserted in our bodies?" Vicki said.

I agreed. Us humans have proven time and again we put selfish gains above peace and harmony. Until we addressed this, every invention and discovery, no matter how noble, would lead only to our doom. Yes, the nanochip could help us to transcend our physical and mental limitations. But given the current state of our consciousness, this would be at the expense of our very soul. Therefore, no, our morality was not ready for it.

I knew what I had to do. I had to either destroy the nanochip or lock it away until we truly evolved.

Gabe turned to Steven. "My friend, dreams connect us to our soul and to the Universe. We can't interfere with them."

Steven let out a defeated smile. "I see it

now…the Dream Catcher will break this connection and replace it with total mind control."

"It won't upgrade our skills. It'll just blast propaganda in our minds when we sleep. It's no coincidence the Grid headhunted you for this project, given your background in cryonics." Caleb added.

"What's the link between the two?" Hemmy asked.

Gabe stepped in. "I've researched ancient prophecies that talk about exactly this. When we die, we review our life and all the good and the bad in it. We're made accountable by God, Divine, the Universe, karma, whatever you wanna call it. What's the only way to bypass this and avoid all consequences if we've been up to no good?"

"Not dying…?" Steven replied.

Gabe raised his brows, wrinkled his forehead and nodded vigorously.

"Oh yuck! Like vampires?" JOEL cringed.

"Yes! But the option of prolonging lives indefinitely through cryonics will only be for elites and not for everyday plebs like us," Caleb said.

Of course! If our consciousness is not naturally evolved to make altruistic choices, then only the fear of divine or karma keeps us in check. If we take that fear of Judgment away, we risk everything turning into a cold, dark, barren winter.

"Now I feel really great about my job!" Steven sighed. I completely and whole-heartedly understood his sentiment.

"Who here has not been used as a pawn by the Grid, raise your hands," Gabe said.

We all kept our hands down. No-one could even lift a finger.

"More important is, we draw the line right now!" He added.

Steven took a big gulp of water and said, "The Grid has a quantum computer, which tracks all possible futures. They want to control everything including death. This is not about technology anymore; we're going into metaphysical realms as well."

"This computer's warning us, maybe coz its primary code is to protect humans…?" I thought out loud.

Steven nodded and added his two cents. "Although we can't be sure what codes have been added to override it."

Together we shared what we had discovered over the last few days.

Everyone looked at us in disbelief.

"Clearly, our rulers aren't just technologically advanced. They're also light years ahead in spirituality. That's why they banned dreaming, which is essentially a ban on our very soul." Vicki spoke after a pause.

"They've also joined forces with minions of Demiurge to get complete control. But let's be honest…it's our own actions, or inactions, that have made us weak n vulnerable." Gabe scoffed.

It was true. We were waking up and taking all our breaths in the Demiurge's world. Our lives mirrored his own wound of abandonment. Yes, his minions fed on our wounds and kept us trapped through our unruly emotions. But the greater truth was, AI and minions were just two basic players in this war against our soul. Their real powers came from us giving up ours and falling prey to a few human elites. *Human* being the operative word.

Or to put simply, it was not AI or demonic

entities we were up against. We were really fighting our own here, including our own selves and our own unresolved minions.

I flashed back to shadows and the gaunt face in my living room. Minions had used my pain to play with me. How much power would they have had if there was nothing within myself that was keeping me trapped in the first place?

"Cryonics has to go. Us humans need to accept our mortality and focus on living a good life; not an unnaturally prolonged one." Steven's voice was strong and decisive.

Everyone agreed. It all came down to morality, did it not?

"Also, we need to forget about the AI grid and connect with each-other through our soul grid. We need to heal ourselves from within so nothing from outside can hurt us." I joined in.

"Easier said than done." Divine argued.

"We don't have a choice! The only other option is a life full of pain." Michael weighed in.

We nibbled our food in silence. No-one said another word for the next few minutes.

Our task ahead, as monstrous as it was, was non-negotiable and clear. In this battle for our souls, we needed to fight shadows. The ones that stalked us from outside and the ones that haunted us from within.

Gabe revived the conversation. "What's your plan, Caleb?"

"A civil war." He replied.

Gabe shook his head in disapproval. But his eyes expressed an understanding.

"We've been controlled for far too long. The war will destabilise the Grid and put us, the seers, back in charge," Caleb said.

"What about the blood-shed? The loss of lives?" Steven raised his voice.

"Collateral. Necessary evil." He kept a stern face.

This was not the Caleb I knew. "You've always been against war." I reminded him.

"More specifically, I've been against you wasting your energy in conflict. We need your intelligence, your focus on the nanochip. It'll be priceless once we clean up this mess."

Who was Caleb to decide what I could and could not get involved in?

"Don't you realise there have been more wars and genocides than what our history books tell us! What choice do we have? Either we let people suffer in silence n die alone; or we take to streets n settle this once n for all!"

"Do you agree with this?" I looked at Gabe.

"It's the lesser of two evils. At this late hour, that's the best we can hope for." He looked defeated.

We entered a philosophical discussion about whether or not the end justifies the means. It was going nowhere. We were simply wasting time when there was no time.

I raised my voice and cut through the argument. "Servitium will terminate my contract as soon as I hand over the nano prototype. This leaves me with no choice. After everyone finishes work tomorrow, I'll switch that prototype with an older version that doesn't work. I'll also download our study dashboard onto my personal drive and wipe it clean from their servers."

The whole room went quiet.

A minute later, Caleb said, "I'll wait outside your work from six onwards in case you need me."

"I'll do the same with the Dream Catcher and cryonics databases," Steven said.

"And I'll be outside your work from six onwards on stand-by." Gabe looked at Steven.

Everyone else promised to keep themselves available in case we needed additional help.

"These files could very well be restored from the backup servers. All we're doing is buying ourselves a little time," Steven said.

"I know! That's why my rebels will start rioting from tomorrow night. It'll force a lockdown. There will be a shift of power. And we'll take over," Caleb said.

"Just one last question, Caleb. Do you know who killed Karon?" Vicki asked.

"I don't. But I can guess. EMMA."

"It finally makes sense," Krishna said. He had been unusually quiet throughout our heated discussion. The calmness in his voice at a turbulent time like this surprised us all.

"What does?" Gabe asked.

"My Caapi visions told me to go away n create a...a community. An alternate for those who'll need it. I didn't understand it, and to be honest, I still don't. But I know it's time to pack my bags and leave."

"You can't at a time like this! It's not safe." I cried.

"Actually, *now* is the time. You'll come looking for me. And when you do, I need to be ready."

Our evening turned even more solemn and became a sudden farewell to Krishna. We tried to get him to stay. But his mind was made up.

"We all need to follow our visions," he said.

How could we argue with that?

Krishna stayed awake that night to pack up his life and went off-grid early the next morning.

Chapter 17 – The Judgment

Demons have no power if we have no pain.

That night, Krishna packed up his life and left the town for good. There was nothing we could do to stop him.

What exactly did he mean when he said I would come looking for him one day?

I tossed and turned restlessly under my mulberry satin sheets with worries crowding my mind. When it became clear no sleep was going to join me, I sighed and got up.

It was only 0350 hours. I reached for the Dickensian novel on the side table. Suddenly. Mitten's whimpering echoed in the dead silence of our apartment. My stomach sank. I jumped out and ran to her.

The living room was completely dark. All the curtains were drawn in, which blocked any streetlight from coming in.

"Mitten!" I bent down and called out in a low, nervous voice.

A faint jasmine air hit my nose. Hair at the back of my neck stood up. We were not alone! There was someone else with us.

Mitten continued to cry. I walked slowly to a nearby light switch. Someone's silent footsteps and warm breaths followed me.

"Mitten!" I kept calling in a voice as normal as possible, for I did not want to alert this intruder.

As soon as I reached the wall in front, I flicked the switch and turned around.

A woman was standing a few steps away. She covered her face.

"EMMA?" I tripped on a wire running near the wall.

Her cold emerald eyes adjusted to the light. She let out a devious smile.

"W-what are you doing here?" I fell against the wall.

EMMA pulled out a syringe with clear liquid from her green designer handbag. "CHANDRIANA would have taken care of you a long time ago if it had not been for your two blabbering barbies." She charged in my direction.

I ducked down. My elbow kicked the back of the syringe and whatever the hell was in it. It landed a few feet away. I tried to run. But EMMA grabbed my hair and pulled me to the ground.

"Can you at least tell me why you're doing this?" I asked between my struggling breaths.

"Because you are more trouble than you are worth. This should have been over the day I convinced Laura to give a statement against you!"

"You what?!"

EMMA pinned me to the floor with both hands and hissed. "The Grid acts only on evidence. Laura was a willing witness because you made her nervousness."

EMMA revealed she had struck a deal with Laura and convinced her to give a statement against me in return for complete immunity for Richard's rebellious ways. The plan was for CHANDRIANA to come over one night and *suicide* me. Given my role as a senior scientist, an accident or a murder would have attracted the same level of attention as RYAN's did. But Laura's testimony would have dismissed my case by making me appear like an unstable wayward who had killed herself.

However, the unexpected happened. Richard forced them to leave as soon as he found out what Laura had done. The twins, with their loud and flashy lifestyle, moved in immediately after. What used to be a quiet corridor became a party hub. CHANDRIANA tried to befriend them so she could have an easy access to our floor. But the twins were more honest and observant than what she had anticipated. They filed a report against her for trespassing. That was when EMMA had to take over and complete the assignment of "suiciding" me.

"You are a loose cannon! You could have been one of us. But you just had to go off the rails!" EMMA's anger made her shake, which loosened her grip on me.

"But why did you kill RYAN? And ADAM…?" I tried to get as much information out of her as I could, while at the same time, keeping her distracted.

"We could not risk them and others like them coming together and causing problems for us. And you…! You were supposed to die straight after them."

"Why? I didn't even know them!"

"You were about to! We could see it clearly through our quantum software." EMMA tightened her grip again.

The jigsaw piece of that computer in the Grid's basement finally fell into place.

"I have to admit, it was a tight plan. But how did CHANDRIANA get involved?" I used flattery as a weapon to buy more time.

EMMA's body eased. I pretended to cough and moved an inch away. Unbeknown to her, the syringe was almost within the reach of my foot.

"CHANDRIANA has no morals. People like her are very useful to us. I bailed her out of prison and had her enrol in your study so she could be close to you. PROF AMON was easy to manipulate. Sara, on the other hand, became suspicious. I had CHANDRIANA take her out. She was headed to kill you straight after but a dog, of all the things, a bloody dog got in the way and dragged you to a bunch of low-lives who would have created a scene!"

EMMA was referring to the morning just after my Caapi vision quest. And here I was thinking it was me who had helped Cynthia and her dog by feeding them miserly bites! Why were Cynthia and my lives so intertwined? And why was she, of all the people, chosen to save me in this matrix?

A wave of anger coiled me. I kicked EMMA with my leg. Her body became unsteady. I grabbed her shoulders and toppled her to a side, then ran to the needle and picked it up.

EMMA's body crashed on the floor. But her confidence did not. She charged towards me and forced me against the wall behind.

"You won't get away with it! My brother will come for you!" I screamed.

"You mean your brother JACOB? The one who has not spoken to you in years? The one who knows about our plan to kill you and does not care because he hates you!"

EMMA's cruel words turned into sharp knives and pierced my heart. Everything froze including my own instincts that were protecting me. How did she know about JACOB? Also, was she telling the truth or playing another mind game?

In my moment of relapse, she snatched the needle from me and locked me back in her grip. The tip of that needle touched the flesh on my neck. I closed my eyes. A tear fell out.

If this was how it was going to end, then so be it.

Suddenly, EMMA screeched!

I opened my eyes. Caleb was dragging her away from me. Gabe was helping me to get up.

"I made a mistake by trusting you!" EMMA barked at Caleb.

He stood behind her and restrained her with his arms. She kicked his shins repeatedly and freed herself. She growled and launched at me. But before she could reach me, Gabe grabbed her.

She dug her elbow into his stomach. But he did not let go. She twisted her body, and with or without intending to, emptied the syringe into his arm. Gabe grabbed his chest and convulsed. He let out a shriek and within a second, fell to the ground.

I ran to him and tried to get him up. But he laid on the floor without a twitch.

"Why isn't he moving?" I panicked.

Caleb joined me to perform a cardiopulmonary resuscitation. However, Gabe did not even flinch.

EMMA slowly retreated. But before she could get to the door, Caleb growled and leapt on her. He snapped her neck. She melted on the floor.

We tried to wake Gabe up over and over again. But it really was to no avail. He neither had a breath nor a beat.

"Did he just have a...a c-cardiac arrest?" I continued with my failed attempts to revive him.

Caleb took his pulse, looked into my teary eyes and quivered. "He's gone."

"No! We have to bring him back!"

We tried again. But nothing happened.

"Cassandra, we need to let Hemmy know."

"No…"

Caleb turned his back to make the call.

In all the commotion, I had not even asked how Caleb and Gabe were here. Once he got off the phone, he told me he had been following EMMA because he knew she would attack me at the first chance she got. He saw her come into my building an hour ago but was unable to get in. He immediately called Gabe for a back-up. He still had a spare set of keys I had given him a couple of years ago. Unfortunately, the scanner could not open the main building entrance because our apartment security had been upgraded since. Caleb pressed buzzers of various apartments so he could be let in. Only the twins answered. They had heard the commotion as well and were about to call cops. Once Caleb was on our floor, he was ready to break my door down but did not need to as my lock was still the same. The key worked. Him and Gabe ran inside. The twins left to call Steven on the number Gabe gave them.

"Of all your neighbours, only the twins cared. I told them to keep their door locked and not open it for anyone."

I never thought I would say this…but…I was truly grateful Richard and Laura were gone, and PEARL and JADE were here. I owed them my life.

It was a funny feeling. I had wasted most of my life judging and fearing. But today showed me the conflict was not as much between seers and organics as it was between freedom and control. That there were good and bad apples on both sides.

Just then, my intercom buzzed. It was Steven. Caleb let him up. He opened the door and came up to me. He wiped my tears as I sat sobbing on the floor with Gabe's head in my lap.

"Dunno how EMMA's death will affect us. But we can't take any risks. We've got a couple of hours before the city wakes up. Steven, Cassandra, you guys need to act now. I'll take care of things here," Caleb said.

I kissed Gabe's still warm forehead and cried. "Thank you for saving my life."

After a short prayer for his soul, I switched into a survival mode. I washed my face, brushed my teeth, tied my hair up and changed out of my pyjamas, all in less than five minutes. Steven and I called cabs to our respective works. Caleb stayed behind to clean up.

Soon, I was outside Servitium. I pressed my fingerprint against the scanner on the main door. The glass frame parted into two; its eerie creak posed a question: *Are you really sure about this? There may still be time to turn back.*

I took a deep breath and straightened my shoulders. My primitive brain could not manipulate me anymore. I pressed a button and took the lift to level thirty-six.

As soon as I entered the lab, immense sadness came over me. *Was I really about to destroy what I had sacrificed everything to build?* How a part of me wished it was this time last year when I was still deep in my sleep. But the scene had already been set on the stage of life. It was time to do my act, my real act.

My shaking hands and thumping heart were the only two here at this early hour. I entered the clean room and opened the freezer. The creaking and popping startled me. I took the tightly sealed container out, which had the one and only nanochip prototype. I put it in a freezer bag and transferred it in my handbag. I bent down and took out another container, which was tucked in a far corner in the same freezer. It was an older model of the nanochip that had glitches. I opened that contained, exposed the chip to the room air and all its contaminants, and added a small drop of water to make it corrode.

EMMA's words managed to haunt me despite my autopilot mode. 'You mean your brother JACOB? The one who has not spoken to you in years? The one who knows about our plan to kill you and does not care because he hates you!'

Was this really true?

My mind stopped working. I had to take my phone out. My uncoordinated fingers typed a message: *How are you, little brother? It's been a long while. Let's talk.* I stared at the screen for a good few minutes before pressing *send*.

My phone buzzed back immediately and startled me. It was only Caleb messaging me on an encrypted application. He asked: *How are you going?*

I replied: *I'll be done in twenty minutes.*

He wrote back: *Steven's almost done too. We will*

meet you outside Servitium.

I reached for my computer and logged into our study database. I selected all the files and pressed *download. Five minutes*, it said. Five long minutes. Every second brought a threat of someone walking in and catching me in the act.

When all the files were downloaded, I ejected my memory card. I selected everything once again, including step-by-step instructions on how I had built the nanochip and how to override glitches, and pressed delete.

A message popped up: *Are you sure?*

My mouth became dry. I clicked *yes*.

Another message popped up: *Deleted files are unable to be restored.*

If only that were true! At best, this bought us fourty-eight hours.

I clicked *yes* again.

Five minutes, it said again.

By now, my tongue was furry and my mouth was choking. I packed up the old model of the chip and put it back in the freezer. I tidied up the bench. While the files continued to be deleted, I walked to a nearby water cooler. As soon as I pressed its button, a gush of stream screamed into my paper cup and shook the whole place up!

I flinched. Shivers ran down my spine. Was the cooler this loud during busy and buzzing office hours as well? Or did it only screech at intruders who broke in during the silence of early mornings?

"Who is there?" Someone said.

My barely beating heart stopped altogether! I wanted to ask the same question.

I crawled back to the clean room and turned

the light off. All the files had now been deleted. I hid under the table. But the screen, which emitted a faint glow, betrayed my presence in the room.

The footsteps continued to approach.

Suddenly, my eyes caught my handbag that was sitting carelessly on the bench in front of the door. It was my very distinct yellow handbag that had the stolen nanochip inside.

"Anyone there?" The footsteps were closing in. In fact, they were only a few meters away.

My breathing stopped. My blood spiked all the way to my head. A hot flush gripped my entire body.

Just when I thought it was game over, there was a lighting followed by a thunder outside.

"Ah!" The footsteps stopped. A minute later, they retreated until I could not hear them anymore. Everything went back to ten minutes ago.

I forced the water down in one big gulp and crawled back to the computer. I entered my login again and closed the program down. I right clicked on an icon and made a few changes, the last one being *restore to factory settings*. A wheel appeared and circled for eternity. I grabbed the cup and my bag and packed up. When the wheel stopped spinning, I shut everything down.

Another thunder screamed in the sky. Heavy drops fell onto the roof. I hid behind these sounds and opened the creaky door of the clean room. I looked one last time at the pot plant and its flourishing, green leaves. I trickled the last few drops from my cup into its soil. A few steps later, I opened the lab door. When I was in the hallway, I pressed the button to open the lift. In less than two minutes, I was out of the building, and under another roar followed by sweltering rain. I embraced its drench, for it had given me shelter and granted a safe passage out.

I looked back at Servitium one last time. The Servitium that had been a home to my dreams. I never imagined I would one early morning break into it and sever all ties.

Steven came up from behind. "I've wiped the Dream Catcher and Cryonics databases, and have the one and only copy."

I was trembling. He held my hand. We walked together to a cab where Caleb was waiting for us.

As soon as I opened the door, Caleb looked at me with mixed emotions. It was unfair. He was the one who had shut me out of his life and created this distance! What was I supposed to do?

He looked away and spoke in a stern voice. "Our region's breaking into riots as we speak. This will destabilise the Grid. My group will swoop in and take charge. When you get home, lock your doors and windows, and don't go out till it's over."

"Caleb, I'm coming with you. Cassandra, take my memory cards and keep 'em safe." Steven, who was seated next to me in the backseat, handed me a small bag.

"Howz Hemmy doing?" I asked, and wondered how everyone else was and if Krishna had made it out safe.

"He's in shock. When all this is over, we'll have a proper service for Gabe."

"This…this bloodshed….is it right?" I wondered out loud.

"Unfortunately, yes." Caleb's voice was stiff.

The car stopped outside my apartment building. Steven got out and walked me to the main door. His face was solemn and his eyes were tired.

"We have no choice but to lock our life's work away. Or we'll regret it." He held my hand and leaned his forehead into mine.

I nodded and let out a defeated smile. Our heavy hearts opened. We kissed for the first time.

Steven hopped back into the car and left with Caleb.

I was back home by 0630 hours. Mitten, as always, was by the door. Gabe and EMMA's bodies were gone. The whole place was cleaned up. It was as if nothing had happened here. But I knew differently.

I had a quick shower and tried to catch up on lost sleep. Only, whenever I closed my eyes, EMMA jabbed Gabe and he collapsed onto the floor. This flashback played in a loop and left me in a cold sweat.

I got up and went to the kitchen to make myself a strong cup of coffee. Caleb had left the spare set of keys on the dining table with this note: *Sorry I kept these for way too long.*

There was a tinge in my heart. I put the set in a drawer and went back to the bedroom.

I logged online to catch up on what was going on across the globe. Also, I wanted to see if Servitium had noticed the missing nanochip yet. But there was no specific mention of it. Major headlines were:

Riots and looting all over the city.

Fear of major data breaches.

Rebel coup destabilises the Grid. Who holds the power now?

Yes, the news promised doom and gloom at its the worst without giving away any real details. We were put under a red alert, which meant a lockdown for our own safety. My stomach curled at the thought I had contributed to this. But then, the other option was far worse. "The end justifies the means," I said out loud in an attempt to convince myself.

Suddenly, there was a knock on the door. I stopped reading and stared at the entrance. Mitten let out a feeble meow. I got up and looked through the peep hole.

An immense pain shot through my entire body as soon as I saw the distorted image standing in the corridor through the convex mirror.

"Cassandra, I know you are in there." The knock repeated itself.

I hesitated. Standing before my eyes was my little brother JACOB. I had not seen him in over five years. He was the same brother who as a child used to hang onto my every word and follow me around the house. But now, he could not care less whether I lived or died. Or…was that a lie EMMA had told to mess with my mind? For, if he truly did not care, why would he come to see me within a couple of hours of my message?

JACOB knocked again. I pulled myself together and opened the door. He entered my home with uncertain steps.

I wanted to hug him. But an invisible barrier did not let me.

Silence followed. Our eyes struggled to find a comfortable spot. This was no time for something as ordinary as words.

How could we break this wall that had been built over the years?

"Coffee?" I asked the easiest question.

He nodded.

I walked to the kitchen behind. I put a capsule in the machine and pressed the *cappuccino* button. Steam escaped the stainless-steel nozzle. A swish broke the dead silence and filled the mug underneath. I brought that mug to JACOB, who was sitting on the couch.

"Still the same self-righteous self…" He murmured.

"Excuse me?"

He rolled his eyes. "I'm so innocent! No-one understands me!" He mocked my voice and scoffed, then changed his tune to coarse. "Except I am selfish and only think of myself!"

"You were the one who broke all contact!" My trapped emotions spilled out.

I stormed back to the kitchen. I grabbed another mug from the top shelf and took my frustration out at the *cappuccino* button by jamming into it over and over.

"Your pathetic message! *'How are you, little brother? Let's talk!'* Now you want to talk? Okay… sure! This may be our only chance; in case you end up dead tomorrow."

His words hit me like bricks. My voice became low. "You want me dead?"

His laser eyes pierced into mine. He looked at me in disbelief and said, "You really do not get it, do you? Of course, you do not!" He threw his hands in air.

JACOB's tone hurt me more than his actual words. I stared at him with a demand for an explanation. Instead, he scoffed, got up and walked towards the door.

"Stay! Please!" I gasped.

"You just do not get it! You left me alone with those people. You just…just left! And now you want to talk!? How can you be so selfish and not even know?"

My lungs stopped pulling air in. I could not feel my hands anymore.

"You are exactly like those people." His voice quavered. But before he could lose control, he straightened his shoulders and adjusted his tie.

It took a moment. But when I finally understood what JACOB was saying, my whole world crashed.

His breathing fastened. His jaw clicked. His fist clenched.

"I'm so sorry. I thought you were happy with them! Why didn't you say anything?" I trembled.

"How could I? It was always about you! Your stupid dreams, your pathetic emotions!"

"As soon as we turn sixteen, we get kicked out. I didn't have a choice. You know that!"

"But you do not just leave your younger brother in hell and disappear!"

"They were always good to you. I had no idea...."

"Well, that changed after you left. See this scar?" JACOB unbuttoned his cuff and pulled up his sleeve. "This is a memory from the day I turned fourteen. Just one of many! How about you show me some of your memories?"

The crooked, keloid scar on his arm went straight to my heart. Tears streamed through my eyes. I reached out to hug him. But he pushed me away.

"You told me this was from a skiing accident."

He did not say a word.

"I should've...should've checked in more. How could I have trusted those people? I'm so sorry!"

A thick cloud of regret swallowed me. I broke down.

JACOB got up. "You may think highly of yourself. But I came here to tell you, you are no different than them!" He opened the door and slammed it behind him.

I had never hated myself more.

Riots continued to escalate throughout the day. Sirens and people screamed in streets below. But what I really feared was the tornado within my own self, which had forced me to ask: *Was it me who was wrong all along? For, how could I not see this before?*

Abuse tears families apart. The trauma it causes damages innocent lives. This gives birth to demons that live within us till the day we die. No shadow out there comes even close to the hauntings of our own terrifying memories. We struggle to survive day to day. This makes us even more alone and broken in an already dark world.

JACOB's untouched mug was sitting on the coffee table. Mine was standing forgotten under the coffee nozzle. There was no warmth left in either.

"Checkmate!" A Demiurge's minion laughed and whispered straight into my soul.

Chapter 18 – The World

Riots continued to escalate and went on for a total of three days and nights. I remained locked in my apartment where I was at the mercy of my inner demons. The sirens, shouting and stampeding outside were drowned by a haunting choo-choo and a ticking clock. These reminded me despite my best efforts to survive and be a good person, I had made a fundamental mistake and turned into what I despised the most. Is this how the unfortunate cycle traps us and becomes a part of the next generation?

On the fourth morning, Steven, who had kept intermittent contact through encrypted messages, gave me a call. "The new leadership will be announced this afternoon. They've asked me to be the chief health officer."

Many questions went through my mind. I asked the top two. "What's this new leadership? And what's the role about?"

"It's basically a new Grid. Caleb's going to be an integral part of it. I'll be advising the health minister. But I'll sign the contract only if they fund projects that explore consciousness and help us to accept our mortality."

I was not surprised to hear about Caleb. He had the ruthlessness that is required to lead. But if not wielded with balance, the same ruthlessness can lead to one's downfall. I hoped he had not forgotten that.

I was relieved at least Steven had stayed true to

his oath instead of getting caught up in circumstances. I congratulated him and said, "Lemme know how it goes."

As soon as we ended the call, Caleb rang me. He wanted to discuss the nanochip.

"We need to suspend it. Otherwise, we'll become permanent slaves to our own technology." It pained me to say this. But I was adamant.

He put up a minor resistance. "We can't disregard it completely. We just need to pace ourselves. Will you be our scientific advisor?"

"Thanks. But to be honest, I need a break." I declined the offer and suggested some trusted names from Servitium.

"It's coz of JACOB, isn't it?"

I did not say a word.

He cleared his throat and said, "Look, I was gonna wait to tell you this...but... JACOB's not a criminal. At the end of the day, he was just another pawn like the rest of us."

I remained quiet.

"He'll be preparing us for the inevitable human and machine cohabitation. We need all the best minds on our side, Cassandra. We don't need them against us."

"Clearly you know my brother better than I do." There was a lump in my throat.

This time, it was Caleb who became quiet. After a long pause, he said, "I'll help you both figure things out."

I thanked him and ended the call.

JACOB weighed heavily on my soul. Or...was it the guilt from my own blind eyes? To escape this burden, my old self would have distracted herself either with lab work or data analysis or a meeting or two. But today, for the first time in years, I had nowhere to hide.

I dragged my bare self all over the apartment. I studied the wall where I had first seen a shadow. I trickled some tears where Gabe had laid cold. And I broke down completely where my brother had shown me the depth of his scar.

Later that afternoon, there was an official broadcast from the new leadership. It covered three main points.

Firstly, AI was officially recognised as a species that had rights and representation in key circles. I scoffed at this inevitable. This die was cast long before any of us were even born.

Secondly, dreaming was made legal again and removed from the list of mental disorders. I was happy to hear this. But a niggling feeling surfaced. How fractured and mistrusting would people be after a lifetime of conditioning?

And finally, key players of the *old Grid* had either died in the coup or escaped underground or were in custody for violation of the Universal Declaration of Human Rights 1948 and the Nuremberg Code. This shift in power was all too familiar. I prayed this time it would actually lead to some good.

Steven later told me PROF AMON and DR HEATH were in custody and pending trials. I was not surprised; just more sad.

The next day, we gathered at Gabe's and Karon's combined funerals. The cold, rainy day had us dressed in black. It was a perfect expression of how we were feeling.

Steven held me strongly as we stood next to the two open caskets to bid final goodbyes. Both Gabe and Karon looked like they were in a peaceful sleep, maybe even one filled with dreams. I hoped they were not alone and were facing the unknown of after-life together.

After the procession was completed, Hemmy came up to us. "Before my father passed away, he contacted an old friend, JUSTIN, who works in the Community Branch. JUSTIN will get Cynthia off the streets."

We were relieved and expressed gratitude towards Gabe's kind heart that was still taking care of us.

"He saved my life. How will I ever repay this debt?" I wiped my tears.

Hemmy hugged me. "Work with the new leaders and fulfil my father's vision."

I was surprised to see his confidence in me, for it was not an easy responsibility to assume. People do not heal from a lifetime of trauma overnight. Most had actually lost their physiological ability to dream and even scoffed when dreaming was legalised again. In fact, the majority refused to see it as a gift to be encouraged and were signing petitions to keep the ban in place.

Vicki came up from behind and said, "Gabe's heart was in science. Yours is too. A scientific and grounded approach is what we need to make dreaming safe again. I'll help."

Her words gave me a boost. On second thoughts, perhaps I needed this too? Afterall, Gabe had stumbled upon dreaming after losing his life's work and identity. Maybe it was my turn now...?

"I'll try my best." I smiled at our little group of Steven, Caleb, Vicki, Hemmy, Michael and JOEL.

Once the service was over, we went our ways. Steven and I took a cab back to mine. We were packing up my place because too many painful memories had taken a hold of it.

After a couple of busy hours that were filled with solemn silence and heavy emotions, Steven pulled me in closer and looked into my eyes. "We're simple people, Cassandra. We're not made for power plays. But together, maybe we can solve mysteries of consciousness and even shed light on what a soul really is. And while we're doing that, maybe we can also make a happy home together."

His voice was strong and calm. It gave me hope. I put my half-wrapped lamp down and kissed him. In that moment, I knew I had found someone who was meant for me.

We packed for a few more hours and ordered a large vegetarian pizza.

Steven left for work shortly after. I took a hot shower and changed into a purple t-shirt and grey shorts. I topped up Mitten's bowl with some dry biscuits and sat on my desk amid half-packed boxes. I jotted down a few ideas on how to expand the Dreaming group. Also, I came up with the following three recommendations for the new leadership:

- Revise educational curriculum to incorporate quantum and meta physics lessons including dreaming and meditation classes.
- Collaborate with agriculture experts to develop courses that teach people how to

grow their own fruits, vegetables and herbs.

- Legalise transparent and ethical research into the physiological and spiritual healing potential of psychedelics such as N, N-dimethyltryptamine; psilocybe cubensis and lysergic acid diethylamide.

Yes, the world was turning once again. Only this time, instead of blindly getting carried away by its currents, I was going to keep my eyes open and carve my own path.

"Now it's checkmate!" I looked into abyss and whispered back at the cowardly shadows.

Ten months later, today

I am writing the final words of this story while waiting for PEARL and JADE at Mango Moksha. Our friendship has deepened. Sure, their focus is still fashion and parties. But their heart is pure gold and they have brought much-needed balance in my painfully sober life.

I am at the same table where Richard, Laura and I once used to sit. I cannot help but wonder where Laura is today, if still alive. How people change. Then so do we.

Speaking of change...the world is different now, and yet in many ways, the same. We are still divided into organics and seers. But the waters are a lot calmer.

My life's work, my nanochip, has been locked away indefinitely. Us humans have a long way to go when it comes to refining our moral values. We are just not ready for what it has to offer.

Steven faced the same challenge as me. He had

to let go of his life's work as well; the cryonics and the Dream Catcher projects. It was difficult. But at least we knew when to draw the line. Perhaps a true scientist should be measured not just by their invention but also by their courage to speak up if their work hurts the ones they had set out to help.

The Dreaming group has saved me from the grief of the nanochip. It has given me a new, a better purpose, which is to take focus away from the AI-grid and redirect it to the soul-grid. In other words, to connect with each-other through our soul, as Caapi had shown me. The group is expanding slowly. I invite *you* to join it too.

Also, dreaming has revived my blog. I can finally tell stories that feel real. My motto is:

Our differences do not matter; only our similarities do.

My goal is to expose each and every shadow that lurks in corners, whether of our home or our heart; and claim our energy back from these minions. I feel all my early struggles had carefully been orchestrated by some invisible force so I would have resilience for this uphill battle one day.

Steven is continuing his career with the new Grid. He has a lot more freedom than before in exploring projects of his choice.

We moved in together last month. Mitten stayed awake all hours of day and night to supervise our move with her keen eyes and loud meows. Little Luna joined us as soon as we settled in our new home. She is a cheeky, two-month old, British shorthair kitten who is desperately trying to win her big sister's approval.

Today is Steven and my one-year anniversary. He has a surprise planned. I am nervous. But at the same time, I cannot wait.

I have a present for him too. A poem. Yes, what else can a dork like me come up with? It captures our relationship in a few words and is a prayer for our future together. I had it printed out on a medium-size canvas with thick borders. It reads:

> *our love will be tested*
> *by the emotions within you and me*
> *and by fears and factors outside of us*
> *in moments of such illusions*
> *I will fight not with you but for you*
> *for only the truth matters*
> *that I love you*

Perhaps we will hang it next to the painting of spiralling Andromeda and all its magical colours.

How is Caleb, you ask? Our friendship has become distant because even though he eliminated censorship on dreams and froze chipping of people, he continued with tight surveillance. Closed-circuit televisions still record every second of our lives and tracking devices remain in all electronics. "To monitor everyone's progress and keep us safe." He had argued when I had questioned him months ago.

This unnerved me and made Krishna's words echo in my mind. "I need to leave and create a community far away. Cassandra, you'll come looking for it one day."

Speaking of, Krishna lives in mountains now. He has started an agriculture community that focuses on sustainability and zero waste. He invited me a few weeks ago. I have booked a trip for next month and cannot wait.

JACOB and I still have a way to go. Caleb, despite our fading friendship, is keeping his word.

Thanks to him, we had a polite dinner last month. Perhaps time will heal all. Maybe he will forgive me for leaving him when I should have known better. Maybe I will forgive myself too.

Okay…PEARL and JADE just walked through the door. I will have to put my pen down. And here comes PAULA with my cappuccino and her fried, bob-cut hair. "Smile," she says. I have to because it is still mandatory.

I cannot believe this is where it had started one and a half years ago! I was even wearing this same bohemian dress with yellow floral patterns. I had a run-in with EMMA right here for the first time. Soon after, I was chased by Cynthia, which got me lost in a strange neighbourhood. I arrived home late that evening, and as soon as I walked through the door, I was confronted by a ghoulish, humanoid shadow. Regardless of whether I was ready or not, this forced me on my fool's journey. I learnt a lot about myself and stood up to demons that were hiding within me and feeding such shadows. Mitten stayed by my side every step of the way, and now Steven and Luna are here too.

The shadows still pop up every now and then and try to drag me back. But I am not scared anymore.

The road is not easy. But it is well worth it. Therefore, as I sit in this retro café surrounded by beautiful plants and blossoming flowers, I cannot help but ask:

When will _you_ start your fool's journey and face the demons that haunt you?

------ _The End_ ------

ABOUT THE AUTHOR

Shelly Dhaliwal is a natural lucid dreamer and explorer of consciousness, navigating the unseen layers of life both awake and in her dreams. She has journeyed through Ayahuasca and DMT vision quests and has practiced Tarot and Numerology for over 20 years as tools to decode the human experience.

Trained in Australia, Shelly holds a Bachelor of Science in Immunology and Pathology, a Postgraduate Diploma in Adolescent Health and Welfare, and a Master of Health Service Management. Her formal education ignited a passion for public health leadership, bridging the worlds of analytical science and spiritual exploration—two paths she now sees as one illuminating journey.

Through her writing and her podcast, *The Kali Yuga Compass: The Age of Revelation* on Spotify, Shelly shares insights to guide others in exploring, reflecting, and awakening to deeper layers of reality.

OTHER BOOKS BY SHELLY DHALIWAL

What if you could wake up inside your dreams in just 30 days?

Unlock the power of lucid dreaming and train your mind to become consciously aware—both in your dreams and your waking life.

30 Days to Lucid Dreaming – A Daily Awareness Training Plan is more than a dream journal. Created as a practical, how-to-guide accompanying *The Die is Cast – alea iacta est*, it is a simple, structured training plan to help you improve dream recall, build awareness and experience lucid dreams naturally.

Through daily exercises, you will learn to recognise when you are dreaming and stay present within it. Inside you will discover:

- A proven 30-day lucid dreaming plan
- Daily awareness exercises
- Guided dream journal prompts
- Techniques to increase clarity and control
- Tools to strengthen focus, presence and intuition

This is not about complicated methods. It is about training your awareness one day at a time. As your awareness grows in your dreams, it begins to shift your waking life too. Start your journey today and discover what becomes possible when you learn to wake up inside your dreams.

We are living in the *Kali Yuga*—the age of confusion, disconnection and spiritual unrest.

It is no wonder so many of us feel lost, overwhelmed or unsure of our direction. In moments like these, we ask ourselves: *What can I do to make things better? Where do I begin?*

A Vedic and Pythagorean Guide to Numerology is a practical yet soul-led guide back to yourself.

Drawing on ancient wisdom from India and Greece, this book reveals the deeper meaning behind the numbers that shape your life, helping you understand your purpose, your strengths, your challenges and the patterns that guide your path.

More than just a system, numerology becomes a tool for clarity—supporting you in making aligned decisions, feeling grounded and reconnecting with what truly matters.

Because this is not just about numbers. It is about remembering who you are. And in a world full of noise, your greatest compass has always been within you.

www.ingramcontent.com/pod-product-compliance
Lightning Source LLC
Chambersburg PA
CBHW020100180626
46812CB00006B/2405